GW00357840

Smith

Smith

GEOFF HILL

THE
BLACKSTAFF
PRESS

BELFAST

• A BLACKSTAFF PAPERBACK ORIGINAL •

Blackstaff Paperback Originals present new writing, previously unpublished in Britain and Ireland, at an affordable price.

First published in 1993 by
The Blackstaff Press Limited
3 Galway Park, Dundonald, Belfast BT16 0AN,
Northern Ireland
with the assistance of
The Arts Council of Northern Ireland

© Geoff Hill, 1993
All rights reserved

Typeset by Paragon Typesetters, Queensferry, Clwyd

Printed by The Guernsey Press Company Limited

A catalogue record for this book
is available from the British Library

ISBN 0-85640-485-3

ACKNOWLEDGEMENT

The author wishes to thank Bernard and Mary Loughlin at the Tyrone Guthrie Centre, Annaghmakerigg, where this novel was written.

My name is Smith.

That much I do know.

I know also, from our last walk together, in the forest, that sloe berries turn from green to powdery blue, like bruises which refuse to heal.

Perhaps that only happens in this land, where nothing heals, where the faintest brush of yellow on skin soon becomes an open, running wound.

But I do not know perhaps.

I know that the dry husk of a pine cone chewed by rabbits is the colour of death in countries such as this.

And that the silvery flesh of dead wood in the summer is the colour of life in northern lands, where we should have gone.

There are many colours, that I know.

Because I believe that in colours you shall know the secrets of people, which they will not tell by themselves.

Whether they believe that they are the stillborn

daughters of angels, or the stronger second sons of devils, on nights like this.

And I know that you can tell by their colours that people are dead, and objects are alive.

I can tell you that my stove is alive, with its six rings, its ghost feather of a pilot flame, its black and aluminium.

My stove was made by Garland of Canada. I bought it in the countryside, from a writers' retreat which was closing. In a place dedicated to creativity, the stove was the only thing that lived, squatting black and superior in the empty kitchen.

I am alive, says the stove. When no one is looking, I confess, I have hugged my stove.

But that is only because you have gone, Jude, leaving me with stoves and visions.

I had a vision of the future last night, a future in which we could become a hologram of ourselves making love.

There could be three of me, plunging into every place, or five.

Or two of you.

It is my fear, Jude, to see a woman being made love to by many men.

It is my fear, that it is always you I imagine.

You, who almost drove me mad with your sweet aversion to fucking.

What is the colour of fucking?

A dark and bitter red.

What is the colour of Jude?

The colour of innocence, covered with new dust.

What is the colour of these eggs I am boiling on my black stove?

The colour of swollen bellies, waiting.

What is the colour of the bottle of thawing champagne sitting on the old table?

The colour of Jack Nicholson's smile, all sweet evil and glee.

What is the colour of the table?

The colour of uncertain good. Everything is uncertain tonight, and perhaps I do know perhaps after all.

But all these colours add up to hope, Jude.

Hope that I will hear your voice tonight, as if down the telephone from a distant land, telling me that my ticket is on its way. My ticket out of this fiefdom of tasteless dwarves to the land of tall and nobler people for which I have long awaited my visa.

In this land of one-eyed kings, only the blind are free.

So let us be blind to the past tonight, so that instead of our conversation tilting away into the doomed monologues that conversations became in the last days of our marriage, it will free me from the agony of hope that eats at me now.

Hope that you will hitch your shoulders and stretch, and I will ask you if your back is troubling you again.

That you will finish your glass and set it down, and in the breathing silence I will look out of the window to where the garden meets the trees, and ask you if you would like me to rub a little oil into your back.

That you will give me one of your knowing, sardonic expressions. The slightly amused version.

'No, I don't think so,' you will say.

'Just a shoulder?'

That you will shake your head, tapping your cigarette into the ashtray we brought back from Amsterdam, as I refill your glass.

'Neck? An ear lobe?'

That you will feign resignation. 'Would you like to see my new Panama?'

That you will mime a tipsy despair. 'All right. But it's very dangerous.'

That I will lead you up to our old bedroom, my heart shaking the stairs.

Where are you, Jude?
It is the evening, and still you are not here.

I hope you are not late because you are angry. The thought of an evening again sitting across the loaded table is more than I can bear.

I have put some butter in with the eggs, to keep them moist through the shells, easing it off the knife and down into the winded water, melting there like the age-yellow shroud of a madonna, haloed by silvery bubbles of fat.

Now the eggs are steaming, fogging the window the way memory draws a veil across the past, and on the chopping board a mushroom lies beside the knife.

It is the evening, Jude, and the light is growing dim upon this table. It is the wise time of the day, and the fire in the other room is not quite lit, so that it seems there is no connection between the black surface of the coal and the flames that dance across it.

I worry, Jude, that you were the flames and I was always the coal.

I worry, too, that in the year since you left me, I have grown old.

That although my body is young, an oldness is creeping into it.

At the back of my left calf a clump of veins bubbles under the white skin, and my hands, blue turning blotched purple in cold weather, are the hands of my father.

An oldness creeps into my clothes, into the brogues which I spent the afternoon saddle-soaping. I allowed them to dry, then buffed the uppers into an amateur paradeground gleam.

Now they are beneath the table, their softened gleam shining nuttily up.

I confess, Jude, that when no one is looking I love my brogues.

Where are you, Jude?
It is the night, and it is raining.

There was a November once, when we were not long married, when I stood by the coalshed thinking of the music the rain made, because I knew that when I went back you would be in front of the fire in the other room.

I thought often in those days of us being in some foreign land of our own invention, some unnamed northern country where no one could touch us.

And that night, as I stood there in the dark with the rain on the coalshed roof, with the sound of coffee slowly getting ready, with the rain dripping cold on the crown of my head, it could have been the thaw in a land like that, with spring almost over us and summer like a field stretching to autumn's far hedge.

I do not want to cross that hedge into another winter alone, looking at other men's wives and burning for your beauty.

Because I know now that there are women whom everyone thinks are beautiful, and whom you can see are beautiful, but who do not make you burn.

After a time you cannot love women like that.

There are women whom you think are beautiful, but whose beauty no one else sees.

After a time you cannot love women like that.

There are women you think are beautiful from the moment you meet them, and who the world thinks beautiful too.

They are the ones who seek out madness, in themselves and others.

What I wanted from you, Jude, was a little sanity, a little binding of wounds, a little salvation.

What I wanted from you, Jude, was for you to be the fourth woman.

What is the colour of the fourth woman?

A dark and bitter innocence, covered with new dust.

The colour of your shoes, which you promised that you would wear today.

But where are you, Jude?

Tap.

I am drunk, Jude.

I have opened the champagne, and the rain has stopped falling from the frozen, methylated sky.

Drunk, I have put on my old black suit and shoes, a white shirt and a black bow tie, and I am sitting here at the table, drinking champagne and reading Antoine de Saint-Exupéry.

I am drunk, Jude. I think I am Antoine's co-pilot, descending into the jasmine and cicada whirr of small desert towns, our breath frosting against the studded aqua sky and our sheepskin flying jackets bulky about us.

And among those thoughts, tiny misplaced thoughts keep spinning up like rocks thrown by our wheels: of my mother wiping a smear of oil from my cheek with her handkerchief, of the false, indoor smells of lipstick and cigarette smoke off it.

In this little dream within a dream, the smell of oil becomes the laborious, working smell of men, and the smell of the handkerchief becomes the smell of woman, of the glittering, faraway surface of all things.

When Antoine and I land we taxi jauntily up to the hangar and there is Biggles standing, half in the light.

'Hello,' he says as we climb down. 'Still got all my first editions?'

'Of course,' I laugh.

He offers a cigarette, but I will not take it. His hands are fine-boned and effeminate, and I wonder then where I read that first.

Why are you not here, Jude? And what is that tapping from the door, when I cut the tree back last winter? Or was it the winter before?

You will be here, Jude, before the morning comes. I do not care how long you take, because there is no anger in me any more.

There is only the hope that you will arrive this night, wearing your bitter red shoes, so that we can stand in the clearing haze of morning, our feet firm beneath us.

That you will come back tonight, Jude, and make my life coherent again, and vital where it has died.

That you will make heaven of this night, Jude, and bring the beauty of this earth into the day.

But I am drunk, Jude. I even wish you would come back and help me choose different curtains for the other room.

Tap; tap.

What is that noise?

I t is the morning, Jude, and you have not come.

I have just awakened this minute, slumped over the table in the ether dawn.

What is the colour of the dawn?

I do not know.

What is the colour of that sound, from beyond the door?

Black my clothes, and black my feet.

What is the colour of the door?

I cannot remember.

What is the colour of the shoes, which swing before me as I open the door?

A dark and bitter red.

Tap; tap.

What is the colour of that sound?

The colour of your death.

'There is a process,' said Smith, 'using a rich green with tiny flecks of gold. It's very expensive, but very sumptuous in a . . . discreet, expansive way.'

'Mmm,' said the lawyer, who was trying to work out how something could be expansive and discreet at the same time.

'Like your suit,' said Smith. The lawyer was wearing a pure wool Prince of Wales check chosen for him by his wife.

'Mmm,' said the lawyer, who considered his suit expansive, but not quite discreet.

'We want every part of the house different,' said the lawyer's wife.

'There's a beautiful northern light on that staircase which I think demands it,' said Smith.

'Mmm,' said the lawyer.

'Of course we can afford it, dear,' said the lawyer's wife.

I love screwing the lawyer even more than I love

screwing the lawyer's wife, thought Smith.

'Mmm,' said the lawyer.

Smith jumped, sure that the lawyer had heard what he thought.

The lawyer's wife gave him a strange look. 'What about the carpet?' she said.

'Marrakech blue,' said Smith, who was thinking of a famous house he had seen in the desert, in one of his Biggles dreams.

'Really?' said the lawyer, surprising the three of them.

'I know just the thing,' said Smith. 'It will be perfect.'

'I suppose it will,' said the lawyer's wife. 'It always is.'

Smith looked at the lawyer. Unless you looked at the lawyer regularly, it was easy to forget what he looked like. In fact, even now that Smith was looking at him, he would have been hard pressed to describe him.

What colour was the lawyer's face?

The colour of all lawyers' faces, which manage to be both unhealthily flushed and unhealthily pale at the same time. The colour of most faces, in the land of the tasteless dwarves.

What colour was the lawyer himself?

No colour at all.

'Of course, we can afford it, dear,' said the lawyer's wife, laying stresses down gently in all the right parts of her sentence.

'Mmm,' said the lawyer.

Of course they could. Smith always recommended the most expensive materials, which made him very popular with the sort of people who pay to have their houses designed.

But Smith had done very little work since the day he found Jude. Just enough to live on, and barely that.

His dreams of anarchy had almost gone, leaving him a spear-carrier in the cruel empire of other people's homes.

'There is a man,' Smith said, 'who is at a party with his Japanese mistress. His French wife is in London having an abortion.

'At the party he meets an old schoolfriend. Later, when she leaves, she presses a crumpled piece of paper into his hand, with her address written on it.

'The next day he goes to her apartment. She invites him into her bedroom, which she is repainting, on the pretext of helping her choose a dominant colour. They make love in her tiny, squeaking bed.

'"I cannot have an affair," he says. "I am a married man." His simplicity astonishes even him.

'"The Japanese woman?" she says. "Then I will be your mistress."

'The complexity of his life folds around him, with the sound of many small bonds of trust collapsing under their own weight.

'He leaves her, promising to ring, and goes to the airport to meet his wife.'

'Why don't you write, Smith?' said the lawyer's wife.

'I can't think what colour the bedroom should be.'

'White.'

'Too obvious,' said Smith.

They were in the flat of a friend, in a pale blue and grey bedroom.

The lawyer knew that his wife was staying with her friend, but he did not know Smith was there.

Smith did not know he was there either. When he woke in the blue and grey bedroom, he felt as if he had slept in the sky.

The lawyer's wife was glad Smith was there, even if he did not know he was.

The night before she had told him an old Irish story, as they drank new French wine. A story of an abortion, before she met the lawyer. A story of her guilt, since.

Everyone has had an abortion and felt guilty since, Smith told her.

But they had not made love. No one makes love after abortion stories, except those who are too sensitive, and those who are not sensitive enough.

All the rest of the night they lay, she sleeping and he with his eyes open wide.

Her hand on his crotch, drifting and returning, testing his recent fears of impotence, his obsession with thin women.

When she woke, shortly after six, she guided him inside her, and the images returned. He closed his eyes and made her blonde hair glossy blue-black, her white skin olive, with a sweat-oiled shimmering of green.

The bed became a white futon on a black floor in their summerhouse at the foot of Mount Fuji. Everywhere, the careful remnants of the tea ceremony lay, exquisitely strewn.

A pillow book, open to show the turgid affirmations of hefty courtesans.

In the gloom beneath the duvet, the willingness of the lawyer's wife became a single curve which curled and curled about him, at the moment of the clouds and the rain.

Later, she dressed in grey, and left.

'Tomorrow we have to go to the mountains,' she said as she closed the door.

Smith drifted again into the sky, unsure whether he slept or not. Did he? Was that? Or.

The lawyer had bought a holiday home in a fishing village by the edge of the sea.

The house had been occupied by a Catholic family, but they had been driven out by painstaking graffiti, thoughtful telephone calls in the middle of the night, a discreet firebomb when they were away on holiday.

Even Protestants who had lived there for forty years were not welcome, because they were newcomers.

But the lawyer's money was always welcome.

Smith and the lawyer's wife drove there in her Saab.

Smith had a battered and ancient white Spitfire, but it was in the garage, like it was most days, its innards mysteriously inert.

In the mountains, coloured washing smacked against whitewashed walls, and the white lines on roads seemed to lose the stern significance they had in the city. The heads of lambs rose at the sound of helicopters or the sight of fluorescent hillwalkers, then settled again on each other's meatless rumps.

The Saab ignored the rain and the potholes, gliding around half-blind sheep and stabbing the heart of silent puddles.

In a Spitfire, thought Smith, you can't ignore anything. Even the weather joins you inside.

Smith loved his car, as he loved his stove and his brogues, when no one was looking. He loved also the sound of garages, the clear bright jangle of a spanner dropped on concrete.

Smith stood outside the house for some time, looking.

'Ochre,' he said at last. 'Patchy, weatherbeaten, always there. The woodwork white. Pure white, not brilliant, two per cent raw umber. Optimistic, but not overbearing.'

The lawyer's wife looked at her little notebook.

'It's all right,' Smith said. 'I'll remember it.'

She laughed nervously. Above their heads, the sky was clearing fast, the clouds moving to other parts of the world. Needed, uncaring.

Inside, the house was a shell from the fire. A cracked bath lay in the black debris where it had fallen through the ceiling.

'Cottage pink,' said Smith. 'Floral.'

She looked at him.

'Joke,' he said, digging with his foot at the pile of charred rubble. Above their heads, a sink and toilet still clung to the wall.

'Leave the floor,' he said. 'It'll scrub up.'

'Won't it be a little cold in the winter?'

'Rag runners. I'll give you the name of a Norwegian woman who lives in the mountains.'

'These mountains?'

'No. Not these mountains, or the real ones either.'

The part they were standing in had been gutted all the way to the roof. In the middle of the blackened wall in front of them, rain-sodden strips of brown fleur-de-lis wallpaper hung over the fireplace.

On either side of the fire, the doors to the first-floor bedrooms sat, naked and bitter.

'It'll be quite a job getting this ceiling back in,' said the lawyer's wife.

'Don't put it back in,' Smith said. 'Leave it open, all the way to the roof. Take down those walls on either side of the fireplace, on both floors. This is the living area, behind the fireplace is a long kitchen, and above that is a great loft bedroom with a wooden floor, and an open bathroom. You can open the fireplace back into the bedroom, with a valve in the flue.'

'What's going to keep everything up, if you take all the walls down?'

'Reinforced steel joists. Hidden.'

'How do we get up to the bedroom?'

He looked at her.

'Floating wooden steps, each side of the fireplace. I know a Swedish designer. Hillfon. Gosta.'

'No. I mean now.'

He went out and got a sledgehammer and a folding aluminium ladder from the boot of the Saab, and followed her up it to the bedroom.

What colour were her things, under her dark cotton dress with the lace collar?

The colour of buttered eggshells.

She reached up and unhinged the door, stepping quickly in. Smith followed, taller.

There was still a bed in the corner, unmade under a layer of fine dust.

He walked around the room, testing the floorboards, then opened the door into the next room. She followed him.

'Sound,' he said. 'The floorboards are fine.'

'He had a survey done.'

'Naturally.' Smith went back into the other bedroom, picked a rag off the floor, and wiped a porthole in the window.

'That's strange,' he said.

'What?'

'Look, there's a wall leading back from the other room, but no door into it.'

He picked up the sledgehammer and went into

the second room.

'Did you buy the whole property?'

'Of course.'

'All the way back?'

She nodded.

He tapped the wall until it gave way slightly beneath his fingers, then stood back and swung the hammer at it. The brick caved in, with a faint barking of plaster.

Smith kneeled and looked through the hole.

'Well, well,' he said. 'A secret room.'

'A secret room,' said the lawyer's wife, whose marriage had made her forget that such childhood things existed.

'The sauna,' said Smith, 'and the plunge pool, with a patent glass roof to look at the stars.'

He tapped more bricks out, and they hunkered through, both covered in a gritty veil.

Sunlight moted down through the broken roof, showing a row of dry shelves and a rain-touched floor.

They ventured in, unknown. Smith pulled at a long ledger, and brought down a sheaf of cheques from the Belfast Banking Company. He caught one as it seesawed down.

'Look,' he said. 'The date.' He handed a cheque to the lawyer's wife made out for £3 12s. 6d.

'June 19, 1919,' she read.

Smith opened the ledger.

'Christ,' he said.

'What?' said the lawyer's wife, putting back a welfare orange bottle of fifties vintage.

'"Marble as ordered, Stormont Castle,"' read Smith from the dry, curling pages. 'They built the government from this room.'

'They could have made a better job of it,' said the lawyer's wife, blowing the dust off an old postcard.

It was a black-and-white photograph of a woman's face, half obscured by the dark eclipse of a hat, so that only her lips, mandarin slices in monochrome, and the tilted symmetry of her chin showed. She wore a rusty black woollen pullover and no make-up, her beauty unseen but not hidden.

The lawyer's wife took it back and put it on its dustless rectangle on the shelf. Smith wanted to ask her if he could keep it, but he could not think of the words.

'Look at this,' said the lawyer's wife. 'It's a letter saying "Dear Sir, I cannot afford to pay youse this week." It's signed J.'

Smith looked at the postcard, then looked away, helpless.

Against the end wall, beside a pile of mysterious, disintegrating cogs, sat a set of shop scales, a shop display cabinet and an old Royal typewriter.

'Take it,' said the lawyer's wife, misunderstanding the wanting look that ghosted on his face.

She stood in the middle of the dark and dusty room, a shaft of sunlight through a broken slate touching her golden hair then resting on the lace collar of her dark dress.

She looked lost, somewhere between childhood and the future.

'Sir,' she said.

Smith looked at her.

'I cannot afford to pay youse this week.'

'It's all right,' Smith said.

'I cannot afford to pay youse this week, Smith.'

'It's all right,' said Smith, looking at her with a sickness in the pit of his stomach.

What was it that made Smith sick?

The unreasonable fear that the lawyer's wife was just about to say to him, 'I know about Wolf, Smith.'

What did the lawyer's wife say?

She said, 'Take it out, Smith. I'm sure it's dusty, in this room.'

Smith sighed, and began to unbutton his fly.

In the higher shadows of the room, a bluebottle

hummed and battered on the slates, and through a gap Smith saw the sky clouding over again.

What colour is a cloudy sky?

It is the colour of a dead lake, into which bedsteads and bicycles are thrown.

When the sky darkens to rust and silt, it too aids the dissolution of metal, tearing off the wings and undercarriages of ancient jets as they lumber through it.

But when the sky is the colour of cornflower, even small butterflies are safe.

Bluebottles are less safe, because of their stupidity. When they lose the sky, they rarely find it again.

Before they left, Smith cupped the bluebottle in his hands and freed it through the gap in the slates.

'Blaenau Ffestiniog,' he said, to no one in particular.

Smith was at the old table in the kitchen, with a can of fine cleaning spray, a little pot of oil and a brush, cleaning the old Royal typewriter from the secret room.

He had unscrewed the thick glass sides and was fiddling with the cover when it suddenly came away in his hands like a pair of backless under-things, exposing the innards of the machine.

Smith looked at the revealed rods and keys cringing naked before him, and his trousers strained at the seams.

He was getting hard on a metaphor.

A week later, Smith and the lawyer's wife drove into the mountains to see the Norwegian woman who would weave the rag runners for the house in the village by the sea.

They took the Spitfire, with the hood down, leaning into corners as the back end slid away and shouting at each other above the roar of the wind.

Once, she reached under the dashboard and pulled out a red woollen beret and a cucumber.

'Where did you get those?' said Smith.

'I liberated them.'

'When are you going to stop shoplifting?'

'What?'

'I said, you're going to get caught sometime.'

'It's the only excitement I get.'

'What?'

And so the conversation went on, as if between two people who have learned the same foreign language through different correspondence courses.

After a while she put the beret on and threw the

cucumber into a field, sending a magpie scraping into the sky.

'I sometimes wonder if magpies think it's good luck to see two humans,' said Smith.

The house of the Norwegian woman was in the forest, up a lane and then in to the right.

Smith squeezed the Spitfire between the traditional whitewashed cylindrical gateposts, and switched off the engine. When he slammed the driver's door something rattled inside, and as they walked across the yard a bantam cockerel lunged at their ankles.

They stood in the cloth room, comparing samples on long wooden tables.

But the lawyer's wife could not imagine the interior of the house in the village by the sea, and Smith was looking out of the window at the colours of the forest.

What are the colours of the forest?

The colour of childish dreams.

It had been a wasted journey.

They sat in the Norwegian woman's kitchen, drinking coffee with an air of optimistic regret.

Against the black of the lawyer's wife's leather blouson, Smith noticed that his coffee was not black at all, but the deepest of bitter browns.

On the way back down through the forest, Smith drove too fast, humming to himself.

'Is that you humming?' said the lawyer's wife, who did not trust the Spitfire's engine.

'Sibelius,' said Smith, who had misheard her. 'Fifth Symphony.'

As he hummed, Smith heard the wind rushing through the trees above them, and saw spots of light dance off his chrome mirrors and join the dapple in the glades on either side.

In his humming, he heard the rhythms of ancient railway carriages creaking through the forests around them.

In his humming, they burst suddenly into open spaces with a heartbreaking rush of blue water and oxblood cottages.

Smoke, curling white against the greens.

'The mountains are only a day away, Wolf,' he said.

'What?' said the lawyer's wife.

'I really must get that door fixed,' said Smith.

———

Did Jude awake from death at the moment that he decided to sleep with another woman, sitting upright with her eyes wide and the shroud tumbling from her breasts, the way it does in old movie nightmares?

And then wonder what the dream was all about, running away before she could catch it, away down the foreign streets back into the land that was her life before that night?

Foreign streets were what Smith used to make the decision easier, conjuring himself away to a strange city when he thought he might do it. He did not name the city, because that would have made it too real. Somewhere in central Europe, somewhere not too large, with the mountains and the frozen forest only a day away. Budapest, or somewhere in Transylvania.

But no, he said he was not going to name names. One of these days he would stick to his principles.

As he walked back from the wine shop with a

bottle of something red and raw, he squeezed his eyes almost shut, turning the unfocused neon signs – Fun Factory, Carpetland, Abba Taxis – into foreign symbols in a language whose syntax he could not even begin to deconstruct.

On the corner above the fast food shop the old clock was stopped at ten to four. That helped, too.

In the evening they drank the country wine and smoked Lebanese gold, taking turns to roll it in a Rizla machine and letting their fingers touch as they handed the joints back and forth.

These are the worst infidelities, thought Smith. Not sex, but the touching of fingers, the sharing of fears.

He closed his eyes and listened to Tom Waits on the hi-fi. Stoned, he saw monochrome cartoons, blending so indistinguishably with the music that for a long time after the record ended he sat there, trying to work out whether Tom Waits had been singing about cartoons, or he had been watching cartoons about Tom Waits.

He rose and turned the record over. Because he was stoned, it took a couple of thousand years. That helped, too. Everything was far enough away.

He walked over to the sofa, where she was curled

up below the window, and took the joint she offered him.

'Smith?' she said.

'Wolf,' said Smith.

'You never told me why you called me that.'

Smith stood there, looking out of the window. 'Because the mountains are only a day away.'

At the top of the window the raindrops queued, waiting for release and envying the way the smoke drifted inside, high and free in the shadows of the ceiling.

'Smith?' said Wolf.

'Wolf,' said Smith.

'Stay with me tonight.'

He was glad that she had asked, and not him.

They sat for a long time after that. He did not know what she was thinking, but he was pretending he could still go home.

On the bed she knelt before him, her dress sweeping off her head with Moscow grace.

Her underthings were white, and the brassiere which he unhooked one-handed, freeing her breasts for his tongue, was also white.

She came five times, dimples of noise in the mattress of the night, then slept. He counted the times, as men still do, saving them for ancient bar-room conversations.

At dawn she woke and bade him kneel, throwing a garland of white silk across her brown shoulder. He told her this, speaking only to hear her voice.

'You make everything beautiful, Smith,' she said. 'You had given too much, to receive nothing.'

'To give is to receive the pleasure of giving,' he said. Wolf laughed. She knew the ridiculous when she heard it.

She slept again. It was too hot for clothes, and against the white triangle of skin, her hair was as black and shocking as burning tyres on snow.

It was too hot for Wolf. She slept edgily, small wolf snarls escaping from deep in her throat.

Smith lay awake, thinking. The mountains are only a day away, Wolf, he thought. In the mountains you will sleep silently, your skin rimed in the shadows of firs, the jewels of frost on it slowly tilting with the great silent turning of the stars.

And sleeping within that rhythm of the turning world, the tiny rhythm of your fisting and unfisting heart, of your breathing, of your dreams.

What are you, Wolf?

You are an animal, Wolf. The complexity of metaphysics does not become you, leaving you free for simpler wonders.

What am I, Wolf?

With you, I am an animal, too.

What am I, Wolf?

I am a goshawk.

Sounds at night do not alarm me, nor days spent with humans improve my edged temper.

Wolf coughed.

Smith jumped, then laughed.

In the morning she woke before him, snuffling into life and leaving padded footprints on the bathroom floor.

At nine she left, for her job as a detective in one of the last great stores in the city.

'A man is spurned by a woman,' said Smith. 'He goes away, builds up a great fortune, returns to find, to his surprise, that she is still alone.

'She says she could not love him before because she feared the poverty of his parents.

'They spend the night together. In the morning, he tells her that he is rich.

'She says they cannot remain together, because now she cannot be sure that she does not love him for his money. That night, he kills himself.'

'Did you love Jude very much, Smith?' said Wolf.

Smith was silent.

'**O**nce there was a man so rich that no one knew the extent of his wealth,' said Smith. 'This man had a butler, whom he would often send on strange errands: to find cheese made from mother's milk, or black writing paper with a golden edge.

'Eventually it became a test between the two, to see if the master could outwit the butler by asking him to bring back something which could not be found. But he never could.

'Once, when the master was on holiday with the butler, he asked him to bring him one fresh strawberry, knowing that such a thing was not to be found in that country.

'The butler wired all his savings out of the bank and chartered a plane, in which he was flown to a distant land where the strawberries grew wild and sweet. He picked one, and returned.

'When he walked into the master's room with the single strawberry on a silver platter, the master was so intrigued that he asked the butler how he had got it.

'The butler would not say. His opinion was that it had simply been his duty to get the strawberry. But the master insisted, and finally the butler told him.

'"You are thinking as a rich man would," said the master. "So you can no longer be a butler. You are sacked."'

'Did you need a loan, Smith?' said the lawyer's wife.

Smith was silent.

Later, as they were making love, she on her back and he curled around her side, he held the bone of her hip in his hand, the only hard part of her, and imagined it was Jude he was making love to in the mousesqueak darkness.

He thought of the tightness of the tiny drumlins of muscle on Jude's back, and then he wept.

The lawyer's wife thought he was weeping for her, and she wept, too, and told him that she loved him.

Smith lay there, thinking of the complexity of his infidelity.

'What colour?' said the lawyer, unusually voluble. They were standing in the drawing room of the town house, as workmen in white overalls skirted the skirting boards, damming rivers of wiring with their clever hands.

'Strawberry,' said Smith.

'Mmm,' said the lawyer.

'Joke,' said Smith.

The lawyer's wife looked at him, and lowered her eyes.

'The first thing you can do,' said Smith, 'is get rid of all this furniture.'

The lawyer looked pained.

'It was his grandmother's,' said his wife.

'Is she dead?'

'Mmm,' said the lawyer.

'Well, then. And the paintings.'

'Mmm.'

'Complexity,' said Smith, 'is self-defeating.'

'Who said that?' said the lawyer's wife.

'I just did,' said Smith.

'Mmm,' said the lawyer.

'And the carpet,' said Smith. 'The Persian rug you have upstairs is too beautiful for the bedroom.' He looked at the lawyer's wife, but she was concentrating on the view through the window.

'I really don't think I can let go of the furniture,' said the lawyer, in one modulated breath.

'Mmm,' said Smith.

Smith did not win the battle of the drawing room, and began to realise for the first time that the town house would be a compromise.

To match the ancient leather backs of the lawyer's grandmother's chairs, he brought over his brushes and painted the walls white with five per cent raw umber and a touch of chrome yellow to take the edge off.

Then he spent a day mixing Venetian reds and cadmium scarlets and two more reds that did not have book names, until he had the aged, earth red of cave paintings. And of the lawyer's grandmother's chairs.

He applied this himself, using a five-inch badger's-hair brush, then ragged it with cotton bundles, working fast before the edges dried.

Then, with a half-inch fitch, he spattered on pure white, and black, and varnished the whole three times matt.

For the floor, he went with the lawyer's wife

and collected many leaves from the forest in the mountains behind the house in the village by the sea. From all the shapes, they picked seven, for luck, and he made stencils from oiled card, cutting them carefully so that there was a positive and a negative for each.

Using both, they built up many layers of leaf shapes on the floor with woodstain and universal dye.

What are the colours they used?

Alizarin crimson, cadmium scarlet, raw sienna, Venetian and Indian red, chrome yellow, arylamide yellow, lemon, umber, primrose, drab olive, Dijon, duck egg and phthalo blue (a mistake, those two, later corrected) and sap green.

What are the seven leaves they used?

Oak, ivy, beech, lime, sycamore, maple and horse chestnut.

How long did it take them?

Twenty-seven days.

What did it look like when it was finished and varnished?

Like the floor of heaven, in the first week of October.

What did the lawyer say?

'Mmm.'

'Jesus God, Smith,' said the lawyer's wife. 'You

have a greatness in you.'

'We all have a greatness in us,' said Smith, 'but it does not come from designing rooms.'

Secretly, though, he was pleased.

Smith sat at the old table in the kitchen.

Until the lawyer pays me, he thought, I am the poorest interior designer in the world.

But since he was pleased with the forest room in the town house, he had bought himself a can of cheap beer on the way home.

And now, in the darkness of the evening, in the yellow warm of the kitchen, he sat at the scrubbed table with a dark, nutty half-loaf, a pot of butter, a jar of grainy mustard, a twisted wedge of ancient Cheddar on a thick and narrow breadboard, a single knife, the can of beer, an old glass with *Wilkins* stamped on the bottom, and a copy of *Biggles Forms a Syndicate*, which he had just finished.

It was a fine feeling, easing back the ringpull with the sound that sounds like anticipation, gurgling the beer into the glass and then setting the can down with a hollow clunk and just sitting there for a second, looking at the squat and honeyed column before wrapping his hand around the misted glass and bringing the cold and foaming head to his lips.

I am the man in all the beer advertisements, Smith thought. But if someone stopped me at this moment I would kill them. Blood all over the kitchen, and the cheese ruined.

That first long swallow was a third of the beer gone, and he kept the rest for the bread and cheese, taking thick slices of bread because bread was cheap, and thin slices of cheese because cheese was not. And then a beautiful crescent sliver of mustard, just enough so that the jar would last another night.

Just until the lawyer pays me, Smith thought. But I will not ask for money before then. I have no interest, any more. All I need is enough to live from day to day, and to buy cheap beer once in a while.

As he was lifting the can to throw it in the bin, he found that there was about an inch left, and drank it down.

'There's something to be said for amnesia,' he said.

While the kettle was boiling he wrapped the cheese carefully and put it in the fridge. The fridge was not working at the moment. For the last year he had been putting nothing in the door, to save the hinges, but it was the motor which had broken down.

Smith reached around the back and fiddled about, and the motor gave a friendly hrnnnnn and started up again. One of these days he would get it fixed properly.

He used half the kettleful to wash the glass, the knife and the board, and kept the rest for his face.

Then he brushed his teeth, carefully avoiding his left upper incisor where it joined his gum. He pulled back his upper lip and looked at it in the mirror.

'You're falling apart, Smith,' he said to the mirror, then spat in the sink.

Outside the bathroom he stopped at the door of the old bedroom, then turned away and opened the door of the after bedroom. He was in no mood for memories tonight.

In bed he read for an hour. He was reading André Gide's *The Immoralist*, which he had bought from a secondhand bookshop in the city. He was not enjoying it much, but felt an obligation to finish it, since André Gide had taken the trouble to.

Sometimes, instead of reading, he would lie in

bed and wonder, if he was transported to the past, what he would bring back to the present to make him fabulously wealthy.

What could he buy? Land, classic cars, gold, paintings? Money would be no use.

He could give Shakespeare a copy of *Hamlet* before he wrote it. Save him all that torture.

Even as Smith thought, he could feel his guts exploding inside him, after the cheese and beer. It's no use dreaming of immortality, he thought. It's best without the *t* in the middle.

He lay there, tired of Gide, and after a while imagined that he was walking up the lane to Van Gogh's house. Vincent was standing outside, his hair unusually neat, finishing off one of his sunflowers.

He stepped back to look at it, then tore it off the easel, threw it at his feet and spat at it.

If I had a million pounds, Smith thought, I could live like a lord on the interest. But who would want to live like a lord? No creativity, no instinct there, except shipping-in toothless lions to stop the family seat crumbling under your arse. Knights and squires, the language of dark armour and ringing glades, defiled by age.

Knight. Someone who has contributed handsomely to the governing party's funds. Squire.

What you are called by an incompetent mechanic as he hands you the oily scrap of paper on which is written the bill for failing to fix the Spitfire.

Oil. Oil was once the stuff which poured all over Biggles's goggles when the engine of the Camel was fucked. Now it was what made Arabs fatter. His private lexicon was changing in front of his eyes.

Smith had started reading his dictionary again, in the evenings, looking up words like *queach* and *coafforest*.

At times, also, he would rewind and replay the little incidents of the day: burnishing a turn of phrase and slipping it back into a chat with a paint wholesaler, balancing up lopsided conversations with plumbers and electricians, tossing in a nugget or two of *The Waltons'* mountain wisdom, occasionally throwing an accurate punch at a bus queue lout.

So it was that petty wranglings with planning officials over the repainting of the front door of the lawyer's listed town house, which had left him emasculated with futility, became textbook cases of acerbic wit in which he stormed out of the planning office at exactly the right moment, leaving behind a demand which the department could not refuse without its incompetence being stripped naked at an inquiry within the week.

Leaving behind the ringing of unheard applause from onlookers who would that they had dared as much.

Leaving behind a clerk who immediately decided to hand in his resignation and pursue a more noble calling in foreign lands.

And so, when Smith had satisfactorily rewritten the history of the day, he would lie on his back for a while, letting the race of his heart slow from the quicksilver rapids of light to the deep and rhythmic murmur of a dark, slow river, and then a lake.

Above his head, as he floated in that lake, passed dreams and stars.

And then, when he was confident that everything of relevance had passed before him and been satisfactorily resolved, he would turn on his side, curl up his knees a little, and bunch his pillow under his chin.

Smith's pillow was made of down, but it was very old.

Tonight, before he fell asleep, he wondered if he was rich because he could take pleasure from the first sweet taste of a can of cheap beer or the fact that his pillow was down, or if he was poor because pleasures like those were all he had.

And thinking that, Smith passed into sleep.

Across the city, the lawyer's wife was in bed with the lawyer.

'The forest room is so beautiful,' said the lawyer's wife.

'Is there something going on between you and Smith?' said the lawyer.

'No.'

'He doesn't seem very happy.'

'If your wife had killed herself, you wouldn't be very happy either.'

'Mmm.'

The lawyer's wife got out of bed and went to the bathroom to cry a little. Then she came back and got into bed.

'Why did she kill herself?' said the lawyer.

'She was insane,' said the lawyer's wife.

Smith had first met the lawyer's wife in a café in the city.

He was sitting in the café alone, drinking black coffee with no sugar, many thoughts passing across the tundra of his mind, dogsledding towards the far horizon. It was almost two years after Jude died.

I have lost the beautiful sense of adulthood, of conspiracy, which comes from sitting in bars and cafés waiting for someone, Smith was thinking.

Was he waiting for someone?

No, but he felt as if he was, which was perhaps why what happened did.

The front window of the café, which was to his right, was divided into two halves. The top half was normal glass, through which people watched skies unfolding, as if they could glimpse their future between the openings and closings of chaos; but the bottom half was mirrored, so that women passing often looked in, sucking down a corner of their mouth and checking their lipstick. Men too, checking the cut and swagger of their eyebrows.

Outside the window, a woman was arguing with a man beside the bus stop, her dark ponytail punctuating her sentences with irregular bobs. She was wearing a baggy pullover and tight cotton trousers.

What colour was her pullover?

The colour of a rainforest ten minutes after a rather significant downpour.

What colour were her trousers?

The colour of trembling seas, in which fish live with a lunatic sense of humour and no image of the past.

The man was wearing a black suit and a heavy ivory trenchcoat, its leather buckles cringing against the heavy fabric as he waved his square hand back and forth, as if practising to hit her. His fingers trembled with desire and anger.

His other hand clutched a flat black briefcase. A case containing briefs, thought Smith, who had been reading his dictionary the night before. He imagined lawyers turning away from the jury, pulling things out from the dry papers for a lachrymose sniff.

A bus slid in. The man got on it, and the woman walked away.

Everywhere the world wrestles with its shadow, thought Smith. Where had he read that?

He was still thinking about lawyers when the door flapped and a blonde woman shouldered in, spilling an armful of apologies. She apologised to the elderly man at the first table for almost knocking over his tea, to the woman at the second table for knocking over her umbrella, to either the mongrel whose tail she tramped on at the third table or its owner. It was difficult to tell which, since her apology and the dog's hurt yap collided head on and ricocheted separately into the helpful bosoms of the waitress whose way she was blocking, and to whom she also apologised.

She flumped into the seat opposite Smith.

'Jesus,' she said in a voice that must have cost a lot of money, 'you wouldn't believe the number of impurities in broccoli quiche.'

'Hello,' said Smith.

He bought her a hot chocolate, which the café did especially well, and which he imagined would have a sedative effect.

'What do you do?' he said.

'I'm a lawyer's wife,' said the lawyer's wife. She lifted her handbag onto the table and pulled out a broccoli quiche.

'Like a slice?' she said. 'I stole it.'

Smith, who was unsure whether his ambition was to be a real man or a new man, took it.

She smiled at him, with dim radiance.

At four that afternoon, Smith stood behind the lawyer's wife as she bent over the old table in the kitchen.

As he peeled her pale rumps apart with his rectangular, slightly spatulate hands he imagined her husband rising at that moment, in a courtroom that smelt of old body odour and fusty clothes, to shovel a few more dark and lumpy lies into the furnace in which the body of truth burned and burned.

'Jesus,' said the lawyer's wife. 'I don't do this sort of thing all the time, you know.'

'You wouldn't believe the number of impurities in sex,' said Smith, entering her as politely as he could in the circumstances.

'Mmmmmmmm,' said the lawyer's wife.

Smith had not met the lawyer yet, so he did not know to smile.

Two days later Smith took Wolf to play squash. She played it the way she did everything, pouncing on the ball with angry grace.

'Wolf,' said Smith.

'What?'

He looked up at the viewing balcony. There was no one there.

'Take off your things.'

She looked at him, the ball hot in her moist left hand.

'I don't want to see,' said Smith. 'I just want to know you're not wearing any.'

He turned and faced the wall. An inch below the height of his eyes, the wall was chipped. The grey plaster showed beneath. Smith wondered why all plaster chips seemed to be the shape of Australia.

Behind him he felt the heat of Wolf. As he reached back and cupped her naked buttock in his hand, feeling between his fingertips the thread which dangled from her, she slipped her things down the front of his baggy white shorts, wrapping them damp and warm around him.

He turned. Her gaze was straight and aquiline, teasing, coy, all in the same blink.

Wolf won, nine games to seven. Smith gave her back her things, then took her to the weights room and made her do hamstring curls and sprinters' presses until her buttocks trembled, as a punishment.

He lifted a sweat-darkened weights belt off one of the wooden wall hooks and did some squats, first at ninety kilos, then at one hundred and forty.

There was something precious for Smith about the way the heavy steel bar bounced and swayed at the top of the lift, at the cruel cut of it into the trapezius muscles along the top of his shoulders.

Something precious and wasted about the sounds that came from his knees every time they straightened.

When we are lost, thought Smith, there are always the older mythologies, of Atlas and Hercules.

He lowered his bar too quickly onto the rack, shook his legs out, and hung from the chins bar for half a minute to stretch his back.

'What's the most you've ever done?' said Wolf.

'Two fifty,' said Smith, without thought.

'Let me,' said Wolf.

She managed ninety, with the belt tightened around her waist to the last hole and a towel down the front.

'Not bad,' said Smith, helping the bar into the slots on the rack.

'Erf,' said Wolf, her legs uncertain.

She breathed in as Smith lifted out the towel and undid the belt.

'I wish the showers were mixed,' he said.

She looked around, and kissed him on the mouth.

I love you, Wolf, thought Smith, before he knew what he was doing.

Back in his kitchen she forced him to the table and lay on top of him.

'What would I do without you, Smith?' she said.

'Fall seven inches to the table,' he said.

That night Smith lay with Wolf on the rug in front of his living room fire.

Beneath the rug, the wood was black. The walls were grey, and the phone was off the hook.

It was a cold night, and they were naked in the rough-and-tumble firelight.

She was lying on her back, and he lay beside her, looking at her, propped on an elbow and rubbing oil into her skin.

Where the oil touched her, the raised parts of her body caught the light and held it close, squeezing it into points. Her hips, the edges of her ribcage, her nipples, her collarbones.

'I love the way you touch my breasts,' she said. 'I love it more than anything.'

Smith kissed her, their lips rubbery and formless and their tongues everywhere so that they hardly knew whose was which.

'I wish you weren't bleeding, Wolf,' he said. 'I want to fuck you.'

He looked at her lying there on her back on the rug. Her tawny eyes were points of light now, too.

'Then fuck me,' she said. His heart held at the way she said it. It made fucking sound as dirty and impossible as it used to be at sixteen, when even the sound of the word made his groin churn.

She reached down, pulled and swung, and the fire crackled and spat.

His glistening hand slid between her opening legs and came out bloody. He let it trail on her belly, the blood thick and glutinous, as she moved towards him, lifting off the floor to receive him.

'Touch me inside you,' said Smith. 'Touch me.'

Her hand sought him there, found him sticky and wet, left a red-brown pawprint on his shoulder.

Her fingers were on his lips, hunting for his tongue.

He took them in his mouth and sucked, tasting in her blood the dank and vicious sanctity of the lair.

As he muzzled at her throat, her fingers still in his mouth, he felt rather than heard the low, moaning growl, as far away, in another species, his alien penis stabbed and stabbed into Wolf's wounded maw.

As they lay, afterwards, Smith's nose hunted the air for the aura of Wolf's blood drying on his body. A grown-up, European smell, like truffles. The smell of love. Because if you loved that smell off someone, you could love them all.

But Smith could not say that he loved Wolf, although there was much to love about her. Wolf the beautiful. Wolf the glorious. Wolf the tawny. Wolf the wise.

He was sure that she would never leave her husband, whom she loved in a pressing, dogged way. There was that about her; that she would not give up on a promise.

Her husband was a civil engineer who travelled abroad often, bringing back tales of cajoling excitable natives in Zimbabwe to build pumping stations, rousing languid Chinese to spin bridges over gorges in the northern provinces.

He had been called away yesterday to Feldkirch, a small town about six miles from the Austrian border with Liechtenstein, and would not be back for a fortnight.

In his going he seemed to take a little bit of trust with him, and Smith often imagined that little bit of trust standing in meadows mercurial after rain, or on railway platforms angry with frost and steam, in the land where the lawyer was.

Except the lawyer was not there, and the trust stood there like a small child, as if it had just forgotten which of the passengers were its parents.

But Smith never told Wolf how easily trust was orphaned, because he knew, without asking, that Wolf would not leave her husband, and that knowledge kept trust assured of at least foster parentage.

And Wolf knew, without asking, that Smith would not leave the memory of Jude. Or rather, that it would not leave him.

Perhaps if Jude had left him in a quiet way, left him with a note saying that she had gone to travel alone in dusty lands, to find there some old saviour sleeping within her head, in a plain bench in a sun-moted room.

Perhaps if she had met an oncoming truck one black and indifferent night, or fallen off a ladder picking apples from a September tree.

But she had not. She had left him with a life like

a ruined photographic print, one half burnt to ashes and the other half torn at the edge and containing only the single, voiceless image of a pair of red shoes moving in the breeze.

I would never marry Wolf, thought Smith, even if she was free.

She has too much simplicity. There is too much animal about her, and not enough human.

And then there is the lawyer's wife.

She is exactly the opposite.

There is too much complexity about her.

She is far too much human. The lawyer's wife, who once told me if anyone accused me of having an affair to say 'Yes, I didn't' to confuse them and give me five seconds' thinking time.

But Smith knew, even as he thought these things, that they were just his excuses to Jude for being with other women.

'Mmm,' said the lawyer, standing in the door of his bathroom and looking at the mushroom carpet on the steps up to the sunken kingsize bath. The lawyer quite liked his bathroom the way it was.

'A flat black tiled floor,' said Smith, 'covered in a lattice of Japanese oak laths. A black circular tub, standing in the middle of the floor, with chrome taps coming up from the floor and over the rim. Oak steps up.'

The lawyer stood there, his imagination struggling to work without a judge in front of it.

'Walls, walls,' said Smith. 'Vertical tongue-and-groove oak, stained black, so that the only colour in the room is the glint of the taps and the white lip of the tub.'

The lawyer shifted his weight onto the other foot.

'Perhaps a simple oak free-standing bench beside the bath for holding sponges, scrubs, that sort of thing.'

'Mmm.'

'Suspended from the ceiling by two chrome rods?'

'I'm concerned about the blackness of it all.'

'We all are,' said Smith.

'The bathroom, Smith,' said the lawyer's wife, tetchy because no one had made love to her for thirteen wasted days.

'Well, you could have the walls alternate planks of black and unstained oak,' said Smith.

'Mmm.'

'All unstained?'

'Mmm,' said the lawyer, an uncertain one this time.

'Ash? A silvery wood, with the black. A moonlight-and-darkness bathroom, the light a simple disc on the wall. The walls just flat and painted, then, ragged granite on black.'

'What about curtains?' said the lawyer's wife.

'Don't need them,' said Smith. 'Knock out the window and put in a great circular one of sand-blasted glass and black laths.'

'Mmm.'

'A room of night, the moonlight, the snow,' said Smith. A room for Wolf, he thought.

'Won't it be a little cold?' said the lawyer's wife, who had wanted to say something nasty but had missed several chances.

'Triple glazing, then,' said Smith, exasperated.

'What was the difference between Japanese oak and ordinary oak?' she said on the way down the stairs.

'It sounds better,' said Smith.

This wasn't true, but to say so sounded better than anything else he might have said.

'Jesus, I needed that,' said the lawyer's wife.

It was the fourteenth day, and she had called around in the afternoon, angry and hopeful. On the table lay a stolen rock salmon and a Postman Pat jigsaw for children over three.

'Mmmmmmmmm,' said Smith.

Since they both had met the lawyer, they both knew to smile.

They lay for a while in the after bedroom, and slept.

In Smith's dream, he, the lawyer's wife and Wolf were in a dark room together, semi-naked and lying on the bare floor. The lawyer's wife got up and left the room, and Wolf immediately took him into her mouth.

He woke with a whimpering tic. The sheet was wet and warm.

'What is it?' said the lawyer's wife.

'I was lying in a room with you and another woman,' he said. 'She got up and left, and immediately you took me in your mouth.'

'I'm sure it was the other way around,' said the lawyer's wife, who felt cleansed of deceit by a morning of shoplifting.

Smith got up to find a tissue and wipe his thigh. Outside, seagulls dipped in the oysterish light, their cries light and metallic.

'Do you never get afraid, living here alone?' she said from the bed.

'I have an old revolver upstairs, somewhere,' said Smith.

'Once there was a lawyer who married a woman he did not love,' said Smith. 'Or perhaps he did love her, but after a while he forgot how to.'

'What was wrong with him?' said Wolf, to whom loving was like eating.

'He had no imagination. To love for any length of time you need a great deal of imagination.'

'Or none at all,' said Wolf glumly.

'Or none at all. But because the man had no imagination, he was haunted by his wife's past lovers.'

'How could he imagine them, if he had no imagination?'

'That made it worse for him. He looked into her past and saw only the panic of blackness. Then he tried to look into his own past, to conjure images of the touch of his hand on dark skin, or the electric shadow of a breast. But because he had no imagination, he could not imagine having had as many lovers as she.

'At night she would lie peacefully with her back to him, dreaming dreams which she would look up in a book of meanings in the morning, as he devoured *The Times* and chewed at his four-and-a-half-minute egg.

'At night he would place his hand almost against her back, not quite touching the tiny downy hairs along her spine.'

'She was blonde.'

'Yes. Her back knew that his hand was there, and his hand knew that her back was there, but the space between them was a distance impossible to cross.

'Because he had no imagination, he began to keep a detailed diary, as a substitute for memory.'

'What do you mean?'

'Since we rewrite our histories, imagination is part of memory.'

He waited to explain, but Wolf understood.

'And because he could not imagine past lovers, he began to take lovers in the present. One-night stands so that he could experience the sullen, indifferent partings that he somehow envied her, flings with foreign women on business trips so that he knew himself to be different.

'He would lie there, looking at these women and

74

say, "This is me. This is the flesh of a foreign woman I see, I touch, in a foreign land. I do not need to imagine anything."

'He told his wife about these lovers in the distant past tense, transposing them to many years before, even though he might have come from them that afternoon, smelling of their cigarette smoke and perfume.

'But because his wife knew that he had no imagination, she did not believe he had had any affairs, and she was not jealous.

'And because she was not jealous, he thought that she was content and at peace with him, and that made it worse.'

'Or that she did not care,' said Wolf.

'Well, he finally came to believe that she did not care. Being a lawyer, he did not have the honesty to tell her of his feelings, and finally he lost her.'

'What became of them?'

Smith looked out of the window to where a single blackbird hopped and clutched.

'She is married, now, to someone who is glad of the simplicity of the present and the future.

'And he is alone. Sometimes, when he comes home from another dry and grimly victorious case and sits alone in his drawing room sipping whisky from cut glass, he thinks of a thing she used to say to him when he tormented her to tell him about her past lovers and she refused.

'"No past" was the thing she used to say. "No past," he would repeat over and over to himself, sitting alone through his grimly satisfied evenings. "No past." But because he had no imagination, the phrase meant nothing to him, no matter how often he said it.

'One night his diaries were burnt in an accidental fire, and he killed himself. When he really did have no past, he did not have the imagination to create a future for himself.'

'I don't think that's the real ending,' said Wolf. 'I think they're still together.'

Smith wiped his fingers across his cheeks. It was a weakness in him, that empathy made his eyes water.

Smith was lying in bed with the lawyer's wife, in the danger of a rain-dark night. The curtains were pulled, and she lay beside him, asleep in the lamplight.

In the yellow, in the warm, he could see that she was beautiful.

But at that moment he was like the man with no imagination, and her beauty meant nothing to him, even when he attempted to deconstruct it by looking at its individual parts and seeking to draw out the elements which added together would create the formula for beauty.

He looked at her uncovered breast, imagining there some golden curve, and bent to kiss it. His neck creaked.

'Nmnph,' she said, stirring in her sleep. 'Utzsch.' Like the coming sounds of distant languages.

Of Pashto, Kirghiz and Tadzhiki.

From the crow's-nest of the night, Smith stood

and watched those words wink at him, from far away.

He imagined couplings in dusty fields, and the shadows of clouds and leaves whispering on his naked back as he covered the body of a woman who said 'Utzsch.'

Beside him, the lawyer's wife stirred.

'Tch,' she said.

Inspired, Smith entered her from behind as she woke, waiting for the moment when she would say the word.

But when the moment came, all that emerged was a tired and happy 'Jesus!'

They lay on the bed, the three of them.

Jesus looked at Smith, dust in his eyes.

'There is someone else, Smith,' said Wolf.

'Say utzsch, Wolf,' said Smith.

'Utzsch,' said Wolf.

'Good.'

She left, edgy, and he went walking alone into the night, his hands naked against the starry cold.

Smith and the lawyer's wife were standing outside the house in the village by the sea, watching the workmen retile the sloping roof and put in a new window, flat at the bottom and curved along the top, as if the roof had suddenly split into an upside-down smile.

'There is an old custom in eastern Europe,' said Smith, 'to put one tile on the roof in such a way that it moans when the wind blows down from the north.'

'Why?'

'Because it is the north wind that brings danger down from the mountains.'

The lawyer's wife was silent.

'They call it the wolf tile,' said Smith.

They went inside. A derelict stonemason was scrubbing and oiling the floor, and a carpenter was wirebrushing the floating wooden steps to the loft. At the top of these steps sat a pile of old bricks for the steps leading down into the plunge pool outside the sauna.

'Is there someone else?' said the lawyer's wife. 'I think there is.'

'No,' said Smith. 'I am alone.'

'You wouldn't tell me if there was. You could fool me.'

'Of course I would tell you. What would be the point of not telling you?'

'I don't know.'

I have gained the slickness of the lawyer, thought Smith, polishing doubt and ambiguity until they shine like the truth.

He looked at the carpenter working on the steps and felt a pang of empathy, like a twinge of rheumatism from a limb that had been amputated long before.

The lawyer's wife began talking to the stone-mason, and Smith walked down the gentle hill to the wall overlooking the little harbour.

He stood there, watching the glutinous water rise and suck at the fishing boats.

There was a great nervousness in his stomach these days, which he could not place.

He thought of the old postcard that he and the lawyer's wife had found on the floor of the secret room. The simplicity of it. The peace and mono-chrome beauty of it.

Perhaps if I had a woman like the woman in the postcard, thought Smith, that would be part of my life out of the way.

We could say, 'At least we have each other. We can start with that.'

That would be some of the nervousness out of me, to have a woman like that, whose beauty I could rely on. A beauty that would become grace and a cruel nobility, few or many years from now.

It will not be the lawyer's wife. The lawyer's wife will grow heavy and tired, with tiny broken veins on the back of her calves.

It will not be Jude.

Jude is dead.

Perhaps it would be Wolf.

What do I feel now, for the women in my life?

Jude. Sadness, and lust.

The lawyer's wife. She and I only seem to be happy in the vacuum of orgasm. Before, there is a sad, elegant excitement, and after, there is a sad, complex guilt.

Wolf.

Wolf is wiser than I know, thought Smith.

He stood for a while longer, the nervousness pulling at him, then walked back up to the house and climbed the ladder to the roof.

'I want you to do something for me,' he said to the tiler.

After he had explained he went inside and walked up the new stairs to what had been the secret room.

But there was no postcard on the floor. There was nothing except a neat pile of old bricks waiting to be turned into steps for a pool.

'**T**he Albatros squeaks and groans as I climb aboard at dawn,' said Smith as they drove home through the rain in the leaking Spitfire.

'After the rattle and bounce the lifting is serene, through the brace of tall trees with Heini following me, then west across the river towards the trenches.

'No wonder the British cannot find us here, in our little den. Sometimes we have trouble enough finding it ourselves.

'The sky is glorious and cold as we rise, buffeting in the slipstream of older gods, and clambering into the blue.

'In a field outside a house below, a cat is momentarily frightened by our shadows. It snatches at them, as if it would claw us from the sky with a tiny paw.

'In the closing west, I can already see puffs of smoke and the tiny troublesome flecks which will grow into men like us, sweating in leather and khaki as they too try to claw us from the sky.

'Now the sky is clear and blue and beating like a drum all the way to the horizon.

'Sweet god, how I love this job. And hate it, too.

'I think, as I do every day at this time, of my wife, and wish, as I always do, that this war had not torn us apart, that I had seen her one last time.

'We are almost at the front when it happens.

'A roaring fills the sky, and a great-bellied jet in the colours of Air France sweeps past us, a hundred metres away.

'I can see the pilot strapped in the metal and glass, but he does not look in our direction.

'When I look back, Heini has already disappeared, and when I turn, my own hands have already begun to fade on the battered leather halo of my controls.'

Smith stopped the car. They were in the city.

The lawyer's wife looked at him.

'I wish you loved me, Smith.'

Smith wiped his eyes with the back of his hand. 'I wish I loved, too,' he said.

The lawyer's wife looked out of the side window of the car. 'Sometimes I think of my marriage as a silence punctuated by arguments,' she said.

She got out and slammed the rattling door.

Smith watched her walk away, then stalled the engine.

Across the road, a gang of workmen were painting a white building brown.

Ugliness crept through the city.

Smith started the engine, and drove away.

'I really must get that door fixed,' he said, to no one in particular.

By the time Smith reached the third set of traffic lights, the lawyer's wife had already stolen two large Polish sausages and five pairs of fingerless fishing gloves.

As she arrived at the front door of the store and opened it to return to the street, a hand settled on her shoulder.

She turned, frozen, to find a woman facing her.

'Hello, Wolf,' said the lawyer's wife.

On the way home Smith had an idea. He stopped at a bookshop and came out with a small paperback.

'Doi bere, va rog,' he said to the traffic warden who was just about to book him.

Unimpressed, she booked him anyway.

Smith took the ticket that she gave him and ate

it on the way home, tearing it into little strips with an incisor and chewing them thoroughly.

'He screeched to a halt behind the giant truck,' he said to himself through a mouthful of parking ticket as he stopped behind a builder's lorry.

'The engine of his car ticked over sullenly, like an armadillo in the dry season.'

Smith looked in his rearview mirror.

At times he was almost handsome, he thought to himself as he glanced out of the window and saw a blonde wearing glasses pull up in an early Morgan.

'Nice motor,' said Smith, giving the engine of the Spitfire a little barp.

The blonde woman looked across.

'If looks could kill,' said Smith, 'I've just been given a knee in the crotch.'

Pity I didn't have a car telephone, he thought, as the Morgan snorted away in a blue-grey whorl of exhaust. I could have asked her out to lunch.

What were the colour of the words which Smith spoke to the traffic warden?

The colour of mountains that are only a day away.

'Fuck her,' said Smith, sticking out his tongue, which was covered in soft-edged fragments of parking ticket. 'Truly she had sitten on the fingers of the apostles.'

'**S**mith thinks we don't know about each other,' said the lawyer's wife.

'I know,' said Wolf, sitting up in bed. 'And he doesn't know about us.'

'He'd only want to join us.'

'Poor Smith,' said Wolf. 'I don't think he'll ever be happy. I don't think he wants to be happy.'

The lawyer's wife put her hand on Wolf's breast. 'I think he's happier being sad,' she said.

Across the city, Smith was chasing a fly across the kitchen. When he caught it, he put it out through the open window into the night, then stood looking at the ghost of his reflection in the glass.

Smith liked his eyes. In the glass, they were cold and grey and almost strong.

He liked his moustache, too, the way it spread into a groucho when he smiled.

Smith had the edgy ego of the handsome but insecure man, which was probably why he was unfaithful: to the lawyer's wife with Wolf, and vice versa. To know that he was lovable, he needed to be regularly told that he was loved.

Smith's problem, although it could be found every month in the pages of clever women's magazines, felt unique to him.

'The engine is firing badly,' he said to his reflection. 'Motorul are aprindere neregulata.'

'Tell me how you met him,' said the lawyer's wife.

'It was a party, not long after his wife died.'

'Here.'

Wolf sat up and took the martini, her breasts jiggling. 'I think someone must have dragged him there. It was obvious that he didn't want to be there. He was the saddest man I'd ever seen.'

'He turns sadness into an art.'

'Into beauty. There is beauty in sadness.'

The lawyer's wife looked sideways at her. 'You've been listening to Leonard Cohen again.'

'Or Smith,' said Wolf. They laughed, and Wolf was silent for a while, sipping and settling in the pillows.

'We met outside the toilet, upstairs. He looked at me for a long time, and then I kissed him because I couldn't bear it any longer.

'I wanted very much to be with him — are you sure you want me to tell you this?'

'Yes. Yes,' said the lawyer's wife, her voice stronger the second time.

'My husband was away — but I didn't want to take him back to —'

'Where did you go?' said the lawyer's wife, too quickly.

'A friend's house.'

'Was it far from here?'

'Far enough. Smith went to buy a bottle of wine, and we smoked some joints. It began to rain then, and he stood and looked out of the window for a long, oh a long time.

'I didn't know then, but I suppose he was thinking about Jude. And I didn't know why, but I had this really strong feeling, that made me feel — I don't know, a bit fucking crazy — that I wanted to make him happy, to make him forget about anything else but me. I'm sure that's a cliché.'

'He seems to affect women like that,' said the lawyer's wife.

'Do you think he puts it on?'

'No.'

They were silent for a while. The lawyer's wife refilled Wolf's glass, but Wolf did not drink.

'So I asked him to stay with me. And I don't know whether I made him happy or not. I think he made me happier than I made him.'

'Drink, Wolf. Don't cry.'

'He once said to me that those who look for happiness and love are the least likely to find them.'

'He told me that understanding was more important than either.'

'Why do we talk about Smith as if he was already dead?' said Wolf.

The lawyer's wife laughed.

'Can I ask you something?' she said, after a while.

'Yes.'

'Has he ever taken you into Jude's bedroom?'

'No.'

'Zece,' Smith said to his reflection in the glass. He was trying to find an image that tugged at the sleeve of memory. It was a photograph of him as a child, in the middle of a winter lane.

In the snow he stood there, possibly in the days before Christmas, wearing a little coat with toggles, possibly red, and a soft peaked cap, which was possibly blue. His cheeks shone with the cold.

'Unsprezece,' said Smith.

But then he thought that if his vision was a photograph from his childhood, it would be in black and white.

Perhaps, thought Smith, life would be a lot simpler if he had not discovered colours.

Colours like the knotted red of period blood; the thin grey of certain moments after argument and before separation.

The utter black of the months after Jude, a black

lit only by the dark and bitter red of her shoes dangling in the wind.

What Smith longed for was a world in which the only colours were the imagined reds and blues that memory begs from the monochrome clutch of childhood photographs.

He leaned close to his reflection, and looked down at the reversed image of what he was wearing. Tan buckskin shoes, electric blue socks, a pair of ivory cotton trousers, a roughly woven navy sweatshirt, a pale blue chambray shirt, and a tie that he had bought in Oxfam for fifty pence, of Aegean blues, chrome yellows, black, white, magenta and oyster grey.

How did it get to be like this? thought Smith. How did everything get to be so complicated?

'Doisprezece,' he said to his reflection.

What had become of all the people he had been? The ten-year-old with patched trousers, leaning on the chrome handlebars of a new Vincent bicycle.

The twenty-year-old, naïve beyond lunacy.

The thirty-year-old, married to Jude.

Smith could not even begin to imagine what the forty-year-old would be like.

But in the vacuum of the future, tiny images formed, then turned away.

Images of him throttling down a dusty motorbike

to pick up a sweet-natured cowgirl running away from home in Flagstaff, Arizona.

Images of him driving home from diplomatic cocktail parties in a black car, wearing a dark and beautiful suit and a crumpled smile, the passenger seat empty by choice rather than necessity.

Most men realise after a certain age that certain futures have closed their doors.

That they will never ride a dusty motorcycle across America, picking up sweet-natured cowgirls on the way.

That they will never play jazz saxophone in the corners of foreign bars, an icon of beauty to women who are only passing through.

That they will not have four children named Maximillian, Roland, Epiphany and Anastasia.

But to Smith this moment of realisation never came. He was frozen in a Biggles land where all things are possible.

'How did everything get to be so complicated?' said Smith to his reflection in the glass.

Outside the window he heard the hum of a street-cleaning machine going by, as it always did at ten past one in the morning.

Smith imagined that in the country, jackdaws did the work of the machines that rumbled through cities in the argon heart of the night.

'Doisprezece, Jude,' he said to his reflection in the glass.

Wolf sat up in bed. 'What colour is Smith going to do your bedroom?' she said.

'The colour of baby's breath, first thing in the morning.'

'What colour is Smith's breath first thing in the morning?'

'The colour of salmon,' said the lawyer's wife, then paused. 'Just past the sell-by date.'

Wolf smiled, then giggled and hiccuped, all at once.

Across the city, the lawyer sat up in bed and looked at his watch. Civilisation is the thinnest of veneers, he thought. Witness the treatment of the American Indian. The holocaust. My wife.

The next afternoon Smith decided to phone the lawyer's wife. 'What about fur wallpaper for the bedroom?' he said.

'Smith?'

'Oh. Hello, Wolf,' said Smith.

'Who did you mean to phone?' said Wolf.

'I was phoning someone I thought was out, to save money,' said Smith.

He put down the phone and rang the lawyer's wife.

'My husband's not speaking to me,' she said. 'He thinks I was with you last night.'

'Were you?' said Smith.

'No.'

The silence had hardly lifted its head when she spoke again. 'What are you going to do with the bedroom?' she said.

'I'm getting fucked off with design,' said Smith. 'It's just a crutch for the limping quality of people's lives.'

'Who said that?' said the lawyer's wife.

'I just did.'

'You're so predictable.'

'I knew you'd say that.'

She hung up.

Smith got up and went to the window. I should have known it was Wolf's phone, he thought. The phone of the lawyer's wife rings with an ironic tone, and Wolf's is more rarefied and burbling, like the exhaust of an old car in mountain air.

I wonder who she was with last night, he thought.

Smith did the lawyer's bedroom in a flurry of despair, sweeping and dragging and rolling and ragging the walls until they were like earth trodden by many hooves.

Then he dragged the great Persian rug off the floor and hung it from the ceiling, looping it over tasselled gold ropes above the bed.

On the varnished floor he threw many other rugs of whirling peasant lunacy, embroidered on freezing *isbah* days and culled from other rooms that were never used in that great, useless house. And on the walls he hung many swollen loops of silk and cotton bands, held up by slanting brass which caught and held light to itself.

The bed and the ottoman he draped in peacock-brights, and the furniture was old and dark, as it had always been.

In the corner he piled a pile of leathered encyclopaedias from the last century or the one before, rescued from the dead library downstairs.

And then he took a black-and-white photograph of it and hung the photograph on the wall.

In all the room, the only thing that had no colour was the photograph of the room.

And the lawyer, who stood in the middle in a veiled chalkstripe when it was all done.

'The nomad's room,' said Smith.

'Mmm,' said the lawyer, who had always fancied himself galloping across the claret-dark plain.

He coughed, and looked at Smith. 'Are you having an affair with my wife?' he almost said.

'I don't think so,' Smith almost replied.

'I know what you mean,' the lawyer almost said, sadly.

Smith knew that the lawyer liked his bedroom.

He was not sure whether this made it a success, or a failure.

He put his hand on the lawyer's shoulder. 'I'm sorry,' he said.

'Mmm,' said the lawyer.

Downstairs, the lawyer's wife was standing in the kitchen with a glass of white wine.

To celebrate the bedroom the lawyer went to the wine room, opened a bottle of dusty claret and decanted it over a candle, then peeled a peach into the sink while he waited for the wine to breathe.

Smith, who would have loved to see him lift the bottle to his mouth and guzzle, then burp, wipe his chin and pass it around, felt sorry for the lawyer. He knew everything about everything, and there was none of the joy of discovery left in him.

After they had finally got around to taking some of the wine, Smith and the lawyer's wife sat in the kitchen, tipsy and irresolute, drinking tea and eating lemon cake while the lawyer was upstairs, washing his colourless hands in his granite-and-moonlight bathroom.

'Of course,' said Smith, holding a piece of the pale, fragrant cake up with his little finger aloft, 'lemon cake is best taken like snuff − so.' He held the piece to each nostril and sniffed. 'It is only eaten by the working classes, and then only in the bath.'

The beautiful ears of the lawyer's wife trembled. With her back to the light from the french windows, they were as pink and translucent as the scissored halves of an unused condom.

The lawyer walked into her laughter, looking like a man who was hearing a sound but could not for the life of him place it. 'What wood were you thinking of for the kitchen?' he said.

Smith looked at the lawyer's wife. White always said that the oak was the noblest. Like the yew, it takes its pride in keeping faith.

Ash is the lover of the woods, pliable and difficult not to want.

Boxwood makes the hair grow, and hazel clears turbid wine.

Beech made Virgil's drinking bowl.

Gibbons loved the lime for nets and baskets, and Salvatore Rosa painted the chestnut many times.

Elm is for coffins, the last.

'Yew,' said Smith.

'Me?' said the lawyer's wife, looking up.

The lawyer looked out of the french windows, suspecting some old lover's joke. At the end of the glistening lawn, a blackbird hopped and scuttled as it tried to drag a ripe worm from the reluctant earth.

'Virgil and Gibbons,' said Smith.

Smith climbed out of the Spitfire, the latchkey in his pocket, and stood looking at the house in the village by the sea.

It was dark, and the rain was coming down from nowhere. He was still tipsy from the afternoon in the kitchen.

He slammed the rattling car door and let himself into the house, going through to the pantry at the back. By the naked bulb there he found the carpenter's heavy wire brush and a bottle of industrial bleach, and took them out to the main room.

By the time he had finished the steps, he was sweating, tired and sober again.

He turned on the taps at the brick pool in front of the sauna, and left the brush and bleach back where he had found them. It was four in the morning.

When he had stripped, he stood naked at the top of the steps and looked at where they joined the floor.

It will take time, he thought, but in many years this will become a real house.

Then he walked down the steps into the brick pool.

Above him, through the glass roof, the sky had cleared and the stars were turning in the frozen dark, needed and uncaring.

Smith lay floating and looking at the rising moon. He was thinking of the dress the lawyer's wife had been wearing that afternoon. A very simple Thai silk dress in a tartan of greenish blues and old golds, like November sun on heather.

She had looked tired and nervous, as if she had put a great effort into building an edifice of beauty that could collapse at any moment. She had looked as if she could not come to terms with the fact that it needed the painfully complex life of her husband, with its ugly torts and jagged litigations, its unbearably tangled mortgages and divorces and wills and all the failures of other people's ragged-edged lives, to produce one very simple and beautiful dress.

Smith had looked at the weary flicker of her eyes as she accepted a glass of candle-decanted claret from her husband, and had seen that she would never accept that complexity and intelligence could ever bring forth simplicity and understanding.

And he had thought of Wolf, who when she was naked looked handmade.

He climbed out of the pool and walked to the edge of the steps.

The water from his body coursed and tinkled down the steps on its way to the floor, and Smith realised that he did not have a towel.

Above his head, through the glass roof, came the moan of the wind from the north as it bellied and troughed in the small throat of the tile in the roof. A sound that was almost beyond the hearing of men.

What do you do, Jude, when you hear that sound? thought Smith.

I think of you living now on a distant planet, in a stony hut on a lifeless plain.

And when you hear the sound of the wolf tile, you come out of the hut and stand there, looking up at the faraway earth with your head tilted in that old way.

Can you see me, Jude?

'I think I'm going to have to leave Smith,' said Wolf.

'I think Smith has already left me,' said the lawyer's wife.

'I think I'm falling in love with him. He rang me this morning. He thinks I'm having an affair with someone. My husband thinks I'm having an affair with someone,' said Wolf.

How useless thought is, thought the lawyer's wife. But when she opened her mouth to say it, instead she said, 'Complexity is self-defeating.'

'Who said that?'

'Who do you think?'

'An old wind swept down from the mountains into the square, blowing the rain up the dark steps of the cathedral,' said Smith.

'Where am I?' said Wolf.

'Lying at the top of the steps.'

'What am I waiting for?'

'A colour to come into your life.'

Wolf was silent, except for her breathing. Smith could almost hear the thrumming of the muscles at the back of her shoulders. He could almost hear the lolling of her tongue.

He tried to think of the colour Wolf was waiting for, but could not. In a panic, he got off the bed and walked to the toilet.

He had barely started peeing when Wolf came in, knelt by the bowl and stuck her mouth under the twisted flow.

She rose and faced him, her mouth full, then swallowed and began to cry.

'What is it, Wolf? What is it?'

'I have to leave you, Smith. I have to.'

He lifted her up and kissed her on the mouth, the hard new salt of her tears mingling with the soft warm seawater taste of his urine.

'Why? Why, Wolf?'

'Because I'm falling in love with you, Smith.'

'Wolf?'

He held her up.

She was falling.

'Because I am blind, Smith. I am mad.'

'Wolf. Wolf.'

He took her lower lip into his mouth and bit until he tasted blood, and sucked.

'Wolf,' he said, the word coming out twisted and dead through the blood and urine and his distorted mouth. 'Wolf.'

'I am blind. I am mad. I am dying of love, and all those old things.'

After she had gone Smith sat for a long time, trying to think of the colour Wolf had been waiting for.

I am an old man, he thought. It is my eightieth birthday, and I am hosting a great feast outdoors.

There will be luckless oxen roasted, mounds of caviar eaten, cases of champagne drunk or spilled.

Throughout the afternoon, I stand and cook,

taking only a little bread, some soft cheese, two glasses of champagne.

Standing before the pit, over which the meat is turning, wearing an old linen suit the colour of forgetfulness, I look down the wide laneway, and see, shimmering in the heat haze, two black cars stop, and men get out with fedoras and machine guns.

'It is time,' I say into my moustache. 'It is time, for I have become a theoretician in the science of love.'

After Smith had thought this he felt a little better.

He went to bed, but could not rewrite the history of the day, to make it either worse or better.

'He woke once and told me he had had a strange and vivid dream, of being a young boy living in a warm foreign port when the Americans landed, in wartime. They were marines, tall and tanned.

'Then he fell asleep again, farting warmly and silently against the curve of my belly.'

'Why do we always talk about him as if he's already dead?' said the lawyer's wife.

'I don't know why he dreamt that,' said Wolf, 'he wasn't even born then.'

'Why do we?'

'Don't,' said Wolf. 'Don't.'

They held their sadnesses, each to each.

Winter came, bringing many small dooms to the doorstep. Smith's house grew dark inside as the months folded towards Christmas, and people grew alien to him.

There is a conspiracy of ugliness and stupidity in the world, he thought. I should throw everything out of this house. I should sell the house. Even to have one room, with one beautiful thing in it, would be enough.

Smith was not a snob, he was just intelligent. And intelligence is not a crime, except in the land of the tasteless dwarves.

Smith was not wrong, he was just hopeful. But hope had come to his house looking for romance in the pages of old magazines, and had left by another door.

And winter had come, bringing thoughts of Jude.

Winter came, bringing the lawyer's wife. She wore furs and an air of only just coping.

They made love, for no obvious reason. She washed, before and afterwards, although the water was cold.

As Smith listened to her washing, he touched a splash of dried semen on his thigh. Like all random shapes, it was the shape of Australia.

Where do we go when we put perfume on? he thought.

The lawyer's wife came out of the bathroom. 'We're going away for a while, Smith,' she said, her eyes careless.

'Where to?'

'The Canaries. The firm has a subsidiary there. They need him to sort out the transfer of land from some old widow . . . something.' She waved a limp hand to indicate complexity beyond explanation.

Smith laid his head, still and silent, in the hollow of her arm, and pressed the shape on his thigh.

The sound of tiny spiders, walking on frozen air, issued forth.

He imagined Wolf standing naked in the mountains, the snow warm on her breasts.

'The house is nearly finished,' said the lawyer's wife.

The house in the city, and the house in the village by the sea, Smith thought. 'A real house,' he said. He tried to imagine himself with Wolf, but could not.

The lawyer's wife saw longing and regret chase each other across his face. 'Do you need money?' she said.

'What for?' said Smith.

Winter has come, Jude, and it has not brought you back. In my dreams, only, you have returned.

In my dreams I am on the phone to the lawyer's wife, listening with my other ear for the oncoming burble of your car.

Outside the window the rain is ending, with many sounds. The sound of the rain itself, like the cellophane being unwrapped from chocolates in the evenings. The sound of drops off the end of the drainpipe, like the bass notes on a piano keyboard. The shattering of tiny watergems onto the pavement. A fragile, wasted sound, the last.

'. . . some letter to the *Telegraph* this morning,' the lawyer's wife is saying, 'talking about homosexuals when it meant lesbians. He says the English language is going to hell.'

I know this is a dream because the lawyer would never say so much.

'Lesbians are homosexuals,' I tell her. 'The word

comes from the Greek for the same, not the Latin for man.'

I carry the phone over to the window. The sky is clearing fast, the colour of shotguns and buttermilk, and the only mark in the new blue is the trail of a jet heading north.

From far away I hear the sound of your car, threading its way through the fabric of the traffic.

I say goodbye, put down the phone and wave my arms around in case the conversation might linger, still faintly audible, in the air. The lawyer's wife will not think me rude. In spite of her intelligence, she loves the scent of danger which she gleans from truncated telephone conversations. She imagines callbox doors opening, great turbaned men with curved daggers and noses.

You come, Jude. It is winter and you come, bearing a ceramic pot filled with lamb goulash. Another, smaller, with baby onions in vinegar. Wheaten bread. Made by yourself, all.

We drink white wine, and listen to saxophone music.

We drink red wine, and you put on a Tom Waits record.

At the end of the bottle, you offer me a wish.

I tilt the bottle, and watch the blood-dark crescent on the lip swell and glut and finally drop, plashing into my glass.

I bring the bottle to my lips and blow into it, holding the deep and resonant howl until it is almost gone, then cup my palm over.

I close my eyes, listening to Tom Waits, and wish. From the window of my mind I can see the mountains. They look far, but they are only a day away.

You kiss me, love being deaf to the clamour of secret thoughts.

After a while you lie on the couch, your face white and edged with tiredness. I sit in the armchair, watching the light drain from the window and the mountains disappearing from view.

Outside, a man shouts to another. 'It's cold enough, isn't it?' he says.

The Tom Waits record is over. I make Chinese tea and drink it very weak, listening to music from the films of Ingmar Bergman to cheer myself up.

You sleep for a while, your face now as lovely as death.

When you wake, slipping backwards into life, you sit on the edge of the couch.

I ask you what is wrong. You say nothing.

'You need love,' I say.

'Yes.'

'Like everyone.'

'Except you. You seem to need nothing.'

I have ten thousand thoughts, but none graces or defames my lips.

You get up to go, Jude, and we stand at the door.

'It is the music of the night,' I say, 'that makes you sad.'

We feel the emptiness of the line of the words as it turns, stretching between us like the border on a desolate plain.

You turn and walk away into the encroaching twilight, your footsteps lost in the soft snow my dream has conjured up from the empty sky.

I stand alone, in No Woman's Land.

I t is the winter, Jude, and you have not come.

The lawyer and the lawyer's wife are in the Canary Islands. 'At least we can have arguments about different things,' she said to me the day before they left, when I called around to see how the Virgil and Gibbons kitchen was going, with its African slate floor and matching Aga. 'Arguments about whether to rent a Toyota jeep or a Golf GTI cabriolet, arguments about whether to go to the beach or into the mountains at the weekend.'

I thought once that intelligence was not a crime. But in the lawyer's wife it is, because it is wasted.

I do not know what Wolf is doing.

Oh, Wolf, I drive through the city, but the streets are empty without you. An old woman stands on a corner, in the doorway of a church, the veins in her legs bound with crêpe.

I drive in the mountains, sitting on the white granite sand by Lough Shannagh and looking down over the sea.

Sitting on the white granite sand, I imagine the crescent beach opening like a lid and sending me tumbling, tumbling into a warm pool far below, unhurt.

There are many women, but I cannot conjure up their perfect beauty, and their promises are walls at the edge of the garden of love.

From you.

From Jude.

From you, since Jude is dead.

Oh, Wolf. We are not men, we are not women, we who love.

We are the ones who stand on distant peaks, calling clarion to old moons and older suns.

We are shadows and roses at the end of city days.

We are the white rooms in dark winters, and the ice fountains on August days.

We are the silence on the other side of wedding bells.

'It's not the money I object to,' said the lawyer, 'it's the principle. We could fly to London and back for thirty thousand pesetas, never mind Marrakech.'

'I don't like London,' said the lawyer's wife.

She turned the key twice to lock the apartment door, and they took the lift down and walked across the coast road to the Dutch bar overlooking the beach.

'Zijn u van de Nederlands?' said the lawyer, who had a collection of smatterings, which he took out when in foreign lands, like stamps of other countries collected in boyhood.

'Ja,' said the tall blond barman. 'Van Sassenheim.'

The lawyer knew that was where the Dutch Grand Prix was held, but didn't know enough Dutch to say so and was too civilised to mime driving a racing car. 'Twee Warsteiner, alstublieft,' he said instead.

'I just think it would be different to spend Christmas in Africa,' said the lawyer's wife.

Their beers arrived, and they sat looking down at the dark waves fracturing white upon the beach.

Their boredom settled around them like a shroud.

'I just think it would be different,' she said again.

The lawyer looked at his wife. She had never looked more lovely, with her eyes sparkling and her skin the colour of brown eggs.

'How are you?' he said.

'I was just thinking about the house.'

'What?' He looked inside, at the dark brown bar, for a clue.

'That it's always been in your name.'

He looked at her. 'We've had this discussion before. I said to you then that it would make more sense for me to buy the house so that . . . you could buy another in your name and get tax relief on it.'

His wife looked suddenly desolate, as if tax relief was some form of sexual favour.

'I asked you at the time,' said the lawyer, 'and you said, "I'd rather buy a car." Those were your exact words.'

'I've just never felt as if I'm part of it,' she said. 'Right?' Her face was rosy with defensive anger.

'Very well, then,' he said. 'The day we get home after Christmas, I'll have the mortgage transferred to a joint account, if that's what you want. It hardly matters.'

'It's too late for that,' she said.

If the lawyer had not had his temper trained out of him, he would have lost it then. Instead he repeated himself, this time more sincerely. 'The moment we get back. We'll take a taxi straight to the office. If that's what you want.' He looked at her. 'Say the word, and it will be done, if you wish.'

'If that's what you want,' she said. 'But I don't think it is.'

They sat in the cicada silence, hating each other, their glasses and their hearts almost empty.

In the corner, the barman reached up and turned on the television. It was a football match, and all down the empty room each dark-brown-varnished table caught a reflected fragment of a near miss at the far post.

'Another drink?' said the barman.

'Nee, de rekkoning, alstublieft,' said the lawyer.

They walked across the road and took the lift up to the second floor, then undressed silently and lay side by side. Their windows were closed against the cockroaches, and it was too hot to sleep.

After a while she reached out and touched his leg. 'I'm sorry,' she said. 'My period's a little late.'

She took his hand and they went out through the doors onto their patio, and lowered their naked bodies into the cool darkness of their swimming pool.

Above, great clouds were devouring the terrified stars.

When the lawyer entered her, his penis felt like a cold, dead fish, its scales scraping and scraping at her, inside.

Why are we doing this? she thought. There is no love in it.

In her thoughts, the lawyer looked at the back of her head with professional surprise.

Afterwards, he squeezed her hand, a strange, boyish gesture, then went in to lie down.

She dried herself by the pool, and was still there when the rain came out of the night sky.

Her shoulders were a little sunburnt, and the drops were cool on the warm skin of her back, questioning it.

Are you there? asked the raindrops. Are you there?

I am here, said her skin.

Soon only the tiles under the sun loungers were dry.

She rose and went inside. 'We could go to the airport and hitch a lift with a light plane,' she said. 'I've heard of people doing that. Or we could take a boat to Agadir, or Laâyoune. I could go to Las

Palmas tomorrow. What do you think?'

But the lawyer was asleep, dreaming that he was about to start his final-year exams at university and he had somehow forgotten to go to all his lectures.

Smith sat in a pub the whole of the shuttered evening, waiting for someone to come through the door, unsure of who he wanted it to be.

The stout he was drinking made his body sleepy, but his mind tumbled with images. The glory of Wolf's head on a pillow. The feeling of Jude's buttocks in his hands as he held her up in the light that streamed through green blinds in London, many years before.

Before him the table sat, not quite plastic and not quite marble, and above his head, buttery light squeezed through the shutters into the cold darkness outside.

He lifted his empty glass to his ear, imagining that he could hear the hum and sway of the workers in the brewery, then put the glass down and left.

Outside, moths spun crazy across the slate-dark road. In the moonlight, an innocent puddle was raped by an ugliness of wind.

Smith plunged into the night, taking to the back streets.

He was almost clear when the voice came, calling to him.

'Like a good time, love?'

She was small, blonde, like the orphaned twin of the lawyer's wife.

'I'm having a good time,' Smith said. The wind caught the lie, ran with it.

'You don't look it, love. Only thirty pounds.'

'I haven't got thirty pounds.'

'Twenty, then.'

'I haven't got twenty.'

'Jesus. How much have you got?'

Smith took out his wallet.

'Ten.'

'Come here, then. Give us it.'

They retreated into the shadows, and he felt her little hands fluttering on his fly. As his penis emerged, she struggled a condom onto it.

She unbuttoned her blouse. 'Here. You can call me Pauline.'

Her nipples were like doll's thimbles, in the cold. He cupped her tiny breasts in his hands as she bent to work the sullen flesh.

Her fingers sent the smell of the condom curling into the air, where it hung, regretful.

And then in its place came a strange, sweet smell.

The strange, sweet smell of the gentleness with which he had kissed Jude's lips when he cut the rope and let her down.

The strange, sweet smell of the gentleness with which she would have said 'Don't', if she had still been alive.

'Don't cry, love,' said Pauline. 'It happens to the best.'

The lawyer's wife went to Las Palmas the next day, looking for a travel agent or a shipping office. She walked the dustblown streets between peeling buildings, past shop windows filled with horoscopes and plaster statues of the bleeding Christ.

She peed once, in a little wounded hut in the centre of the park in front of the local government headquarters, looking out through a chink in the wood at the policeman guarding the front door as she gushed warm and yellow into the dry earth.

But it was some sort of holiday, and all the travel agents were shut.

Finally she bought a tourist newspaper and saw in it a number for a shipping company. She found a phone booth and rang the number, asking in her halting Spanish for someone who spoke English.

As she waited, the four twenty-five-peseta coins she had placed in the slot at the top of the coinbox rolled down one by one and clanked into the machine. As the last one vanished, a man came to the phone at the other end.

'Are there boats to Africa?' she said.

'No.'

The line went dead.

She stepped out of the booth and mopped her brow. 'Jesus,' she said. 'It is so fucking hot.'

It is so cold, thought Smith, standing in front of the kitchen window and shivering.

In his reflection, he wore brogues, corduroy trousers, fisherman's socks, thermal underwear and a stained Aran pullover.

I am an old man, thought Smith. I am an old man who has lived in one village all of his life, who has never been abroad or worn silver cufflinks the shape of tiny shells.

I am an old man who has never lived. If you had a heart, Wolf, you would come back to me.

He took off his clothes and went to bed, lying under the tightly tucked duvet and reading *One Day in the Life of Ivan Denisovich*.

In it, Solzhenitsyn was describing what it was like to be cold all the time. Smith warmed to that, then fell asleep with the thought slipping out of his mind, like the tiniest coracle sailing over the curved horizon of a great, dark sea.

He woke at four and watched the dawn gather

up his breath in fits and starts.

It was too cold to get up. Too cold to stumble to the kitchen and boil a kettle and wash in the ether air of the bathroom.

Smith lay in bed, thinking of being smothered by warm fluffy towels.

After a while he put a frozen finger into each ear and slowly rocked them back and forward until they creaked like the timbers of ancient schooners riding a swell.

He tried to imagine himself up on deck, but he was so cold that he could not imagine how bad it must be up there, in charge. Instead he huddled in his cabin, trying in vain to keep the heat under a lice-infested blanket.

He took his fingers out of his ears and the creaking stopped. He pressed his warm, waxy fingertips to the sides of his nose, then ran them over his face until the warmth went out of them.

That day he walked in many parks and woodland glades, watching the last of the leaves dance, before the boots of winter marched over them. Mad, mad, glorious and free, the leaves.

The next day, before the bad frosts came, he planted raspberry bushes as promises against the dark winter, turning the soil over in his hands and watching it curl into tiny eclipses under his fingernails. It was good soil, black and optimistic, but he could not even begin to imagine any of the colours of childhood in it.

Smith washed the soil out of his hands and went to bed, although it was only four in the afternoon.

The lawyer's wife hired a jeep near Misty's in Playa del Inglés, where the Ulf Andersson Swing Band from Stockholm was playing from three in the morning until six.

What a very Swedish occupation, she thought, playing night shift in a jazz band.

She looked at her name on the hire forms, and it seemed as if she had forgotten it, and the address of her home, as surely as she had forgotten the date when her period had been due.

She drove inland up the cruel mountains, and then into the lush valleys, where the wind whispered in the banana trees with the bustle of illicit conversations, and in the orange and lemon trees with the silvery elegance of old romances.

She found an almost deserted beach, where the tiny dog belonging to the couple who were putting up a tent in the lee of a cairn danced and scampered around her shadow as she walked into the wind.

They must love each other very much, she thought, to be here alone.

She found deserted beaches, seeking only the certainty of the sea, but as she walked she came always upon a cigarette butt or the cap of a beer bottle half buried in the sand. She held her belly, and the purity of loneliness eluded her.

On the way back from the beach she stopped at a deserted home by a dusty track. A home in which the three rooms had been painted red, blue and green years before, and on the floors of which lay the dead catechism of poverty – the gaping leather boots, the senseless collection of bottle tops, the little prayer book, the half-empty jar of tranquillisers.

The single window in the red-walled kitchen was filled with bamboo shoots and the blue sky beyond.

But all the lawyer's wife could think of was that it was like a Japanese print she had once seen.

She left, defeated by civilisation.

The lawyer worked on, toiling through the long hot days of December on the complexities of the widow's lands. He wore pale suits, and started taking naps in the afternoon.

The days of Advent passed by, distant and unseen on the northern horizon.

Christmas Eve came, as unexpectedly as it had always done, and they sat on the balcony, having a breakfast of mangoes and coffee.

They had planned to take the flight to Marrakech for Christmas after all, but somehow nothing had been done about it. Africa was becoming more and more like a dream to them. Although it was only over the horizon, it seemed to be as impossible to reach as if they were sitting at home, in the forest room.

After breakfast they went to the beach.

From behind his sunglasses the lawyer watched the two young French women who played volley-ball. The firm snap and twang of their legs, the glinting arc of the ball.

From behind his sunglasses the lawyer watched the thin German teenager with the pointed nose, with the tiny breasts and enormous nipples, who walked up and down the beach all day long.

He is thinking that he is surrounded by beautiful women, thought the lawyer's wife, and then there is me. He is wishing that he was younger, and alone. 'Don't make it so obvious,' she said.

From behind his sunglasses the lawyer looked at

her, then he went back to pretending to study the papers he had brought in a waterproof folder.

At one the light plane flew over, towing the Beach Club advertisement, and at three a speedboat pulled past a rubber sausage with six people clinging on, their hair whipped back and their faces contorted into a grim parody of enjoyment, like the people who throw giant beach balls to each other on the backs of special-offer cereal packets.

That night in the Dutch bar there were rumours that one of them had drowned.

Mysteries came out of the muggy air, strung on invisible wires. Unconnected, unresearched, unworthy of investigation, they came from nothing, passed before the lawyer and his wife, and disappeared into the darkness.

'Happy Christmas,' said the barman as the clock slid past midnight.

'It's not Christmas at home yet,' said the lawyer's wife.

'It's winter time,' said the lawyer. 'The clocks went back quite some time ago.'

His wife sat back in her seat, filled with gloom at the careful way in which her husband constructed his sentences.

On Christmas Day they exchanged presents. Hers

to him was an ivory linen suit she had had made by a tailor in Las Palmas after reading an advertisement, and his to her was a bronze necklace and earrings in the shape of many tiny conch shells.

In the evening, before they went out, she touched a dab of perfume behind each knee.

'Why do you do that?' he said.

'It lasts longer there,' she said.

For some reason he felt a corkscrew of jealousy turn in him.

They drove to Puerto Rico and sat on the raised end of the pier, drinking Spanish champagne and eating olives, and befriending a grey cat and a mangy, doubtful dog.

The day fishing boats came back after a brief afternoon foray, and the night boats went humming out under the moon.

They went to an Italian restaurant and ate pasta and shellfish, and drank more champagne.

The lawyer's hair had been cut very short the week before by a barber in Las Palmas, and he was wearing his new linen suit.

His wife looked at him and realised, probably for the first time, that she did not recognise the man she had married.

That she did not recognise what had attracted her to him, as if it was something someone had told her once, something that was on the tip of her tongue, but that for the life of her she could not remember.

She looked at her husband, and at that moment he lost any life he had ever had for her, as surely as if he had had a stroke at the table and was sitting there, his eyes open and the champagne first warming and then cooling in his stiffening fingers.

They drove home in silence, and when she could bring herself to look back upon that evening, it seemed somehow appropriate that the telephone should be ringing as they walked out of the lift and along the landing and in through the door of the apartment.

The lawyer picked it up, and his wife went into the bedroom. When she came out again, he had put the phone down and was turning slowly towards her. He stopped turning before he spoke.

'Smith is dead,' he said.

Christmas Eve came, as unexpectedly as it had always done. In the evening Smith lay in bed, shivering every so often. He had been lying in bed all day, watching the darkness leave the sky and then in the early afternoon return, at first edging into the room and then conscripting shadows from every corner for the silent war on light and what little warmth there was.

The electricity had been turned off for some time now. Smith could not remember exactly when, because he could not remember when he had eaten the final demand, and it would have been at least a week after that.

For a while he had settled into old pleasures, sawing wood and listening to the dark scrape of rooks overhead, lifting his head to see the black shock of them against the early December sky. Then, in the pauses of his work, there had only been the dry flutter of the sawdust at his feet.

But strange swellings grew inside him, testing

him then retreating again. The joints in his fingers hurt, at first in the mornings and then all down through every ether day.

He had been lying in bed for a number of days, but he did not know the number. He knew that bed was the warmest place, if he did not move about too much, and that thoughts cost nothing.

But because he could not bear to think of snow, and of the mountains, his mind stayed at first on dry and stony plains, and then more and more at home, in bed.

It began with lying in bed later and later in the mornings, counting the hours that he was keeping warm without spending any money, counting the hours that he was putting off his first meal of the day so that he could make do with a second.

Then after a time the second somehow went by the board, at first every other day, then most days, then every day.

And then it ended with staying in bed all day, for days on end, thoughts of warmth circling above his head as he drifted in and out of sleep, thoughts of steaming water and goosedown duvets and heated bath towels humming across his icy bedroom like bees caught far from home late in the afternoon.

And now it was Christmas Eve and he lay there, delaying the trip to the toilet for as long as possible before he finally slid out of bed and went to the bathroom, unsure whether to walk quickly because he would get there faster or to go slowly because moving air was colder.

He peed, feeling the stinking warmth gush out of him, then returned to the bedroom, lying quite still until he was sure he could feel no draughts, then starting to breathe again, in little gushes and gasps.

I am a downhill skier, he thought. I am a downhill skier, and that is why it is so cold. My ears are filled with the sound of cowbells and the strange, barking coughs of my supporters. My thighs, as broad and flat as aircraft carriers, are burning, and although it is well below freezing, my body is filled with a glorious heat which is half victory, half exhaustion. I blur across the finishing line and sweep to a halt, exulting in the flames which consume me.

But Smith could no longer imagine the flames warm, and after a while he realised that the coughing was his own.

Then he realised that the cowbells had not stopped ringing.

The telephone, he thought. It is the telephone ringing. I thought it had been cut off as well. But then there have been no phone calls, so perhaps there has been no bill.

He tried to think, but could not remember eating the phone bill.

Perhaps if I just stay here it will stop, he thought, and then I won't have to get out of bed.

Stay here, said his body, please stay here. It is a wrong number, said his mind, it is someone looking for money.

Answer it, said his heart. Answer me, said the phone.

'Smith?' said the voice on the other end, when he finally lifted the icy Bakelite. 'Smith?'

Smith looked at his dark living room window, trying to remember what it was people said when they picked up telephones.

The window was dirty, and there was so little light that all he could see was a distant and vaguely familiar reflection peering back at him.

Smith looked at his reflection, and tried to see who it was standing beside him, out there in the snow.

But in the darkness, he could only guess.

'Jude?' he said.

There was a woman once, in a story Smith had been told, who went to bed with flu and woke up with an infection on the surface of her brain. She came out of hospital a skeleton with a memory that had caved in.

When her family visited her, they had to phone ahead and tell her their names, which she wrote down and checked against a list they passed through the letterbox when they arrived.

After a year her husband decided to treat her to a surprise, and booked a flight to Paris to see her favourite sister.

He did not tell her where they were going, and on the flight she panicked, convinced she was being kidnapped.

At Paris he got her off the plane, into a taxi and as far as her sister's home, but she would not get out of the car.

He went into the house and got her sister, who came out and opened the taxi door to find a whimpering skeleton on the back seat.

The skeleton looked up, its eyes hysterical.

'Who *are* you?' it said.

At that moment, looking out into the darkness, Smith did not know whether he was the sister or the skeleton.

And he could not see, try as he might, who was out there beside him.

'Who was it who told you that Smith was dead?' said the lawyer's wife.

'It was a woman. She said it was an accident. She didn't give her name.'

'Wolf,' said the lawyer's wife.

'What?'

'It must have been Wolf.'

'Who is Wolf?'

'I went shoplifting one day, and she was the store detective. When she asked if I wanted to phone anyone I said Smith.'

It must be the baby, thought the lawyer. We will have to go home soon, where the psychiatrists are better.

I am in a land far away, thought Smith. I am near the mountains, and near where the moon sleeps on water. There are bells, in the soft gold air.

I have been away for many years, waiting, and now I am hearing a voice in the language of my people, telling me that the mountains are only a day away, and that it is not as cold there as I once feared.

Hello, says the voice. A word I remember, from a time before.

'Wolf,' said Smith. 'Wolf.' The sound hung, fur-rimmed, in the still air, uncertain, unwilling to escape from the bouquet of lukewarm breath which formed it.

'Wolf,' said Smith, over and over again, until the monochrome darkness of the room was filled with little wolves, holding, waiting, watching.

'Smith,' said Wolf, 'oh, Smith.'

'Do you need somewhere to stay for the night, Wolf?'

'I can't, Smith. I'm with my husband and his friends.'

'It's Christmas Eve, Wolf.'

'I know. I know that.' There was silence for a while, then he could hear her putting coins in.

'I am in the bar of a hotel, not far away,' she said, before Smith realised that he had not asked a question. There was silence again, while he tried to work things out.

'I wish you could, Wolf.'

'So do I.'

Silence again.

'Do you think it's just sex between us, Smith?'

'It might be if we were younger, but you need more than that when you're older and more . . .'

'Sensible,' she said. That old, smouldering laugh padded down the phone to him.

'I wish I could,' she said again. How strong her voice was. That simple statement of fact, with not a plaintive note in it.

'I'll leave the door open,' said Smith. 'I'll leave all the doors open, and the windows, too.'

'Smith, I – ' The line crackled, an electrical storm caused by the relentless ghosts of postmistress operators on tiny isles, and then went dead.

Smith put the phone down, and it was only then he realised that he was burning from head to toe.

'Wolf,' he said. 'Wolf. Jesus.'

He went to the bathroom and turned on the cold tap, which was slightly warmer than the hot, and washed himself under the stinging flow, splashing the water over his stony ribs and humming and gasping. He tried to wash his hair as well but gave up halfway through because the water was painful on his head. When he stood up to dry himself with a damp towel, he staggered and almost slipped.

He shaved, not very successfully, by the light of a candle in front of a small mirror, then hunted out a dusty black suit, a not very clean white shirt and a black tie, and put them on.

He threw on an old overcoat and plunged into the hurtling night, leaving all the doors and windows open and walking the knotted streets until he found a well-to-do off-licence with no sign of an alarm bell on the white brick walls.

All over the city the bells were chiming midnight as Smith tapped a half-brick politely through a corner of the front window and liberated two bottles of creditable champagne.

He walked home through the snow, his hair wild and matted with soap and the bottles swinging cold in his hands, and tiptoed into his home, then leaped through the open door into the kitchen.

The table stared at him, blank. There was no one there.

A fire, he thought. I need a fire.

He left the bottles on the back step, then was halfway to the coalshed when he realised that Wolf might trip over them in the darkness when she came in.

He returned and put them on the windowsill, and was almost at the coalshed when he realised there was no coal.

He stood there for a minute, his eyes moving and blinking in the falling flakes, as he thought of what he could burn. Then he smiled dimly, parting the darkness.

He went into the kitchen and lifted a key off a row of hooks by the Canadian oven, and walked past the living room, then turned right and un-locked the door in front of him.

After five trips to the living room he had enough. He started with the first few pages of the Anna Maria Garthwaite, then added the cover, which he had never liked, and watched as it blackened and curled before igniting with a flatulent, resentful pop.

The purple Lee Jofa was next, its cover turning as it burned into ghost tulips of lilac and gold, trumpeting into the black.

Then the Coles textured vinyl, which twisted itself into the shape of a warted toad, its mouth open in agony as flames burst from its empty eyes.

And the Laura Ashley volumes one to five, the Colefax Fowler and the Osborne and Little. All of them useful at last.

Smith stacked the lot in the grate, the cloth and wallpaper and paint samples sparking and spiralling up the black flue.

He held his hands to the flames until they scorched, then rubbed the heat into his face and through his soapy hair.

'Drink,' he said. 'Drink and heat and Wolf.'

He went and got one of the bottles off the windowsill outside and sent the cork sailing up into the twisting snow, then lost his nerve and stood flat against the wall as it came tumbling down again.

'Ha, you little bastard,' he said, picking up the cork and swaying as he scratched his nose with it. Easy. When had he last eaten? Tuesday, or?

He put the cork in the pocket of his jacket and went back to the living room, standing with his back to the blaze and raising the bottle to his dry lips.

I am an urchin, he thought, an urchin who rides across America on the engines of great freight trains, my shoulderblades on fire and my nose blue.

He flung a *World of Interiors* back issue on the flames and went out to make sure all the doors were still open, then returned and sat again.

He dozed, and woke, unsure whether he had dreamt of noises outside, or been woken by them. He went outside to check, and found nothing.

Cars approached, slowed, then accelerated away, mocking him. He heard shadows drag themselves across the ground outside. He heard leaves fall, and his half-awake imagination turned the haloed echoes of their falling into the shape of wolfprints.

At some time in the night, which he imagined to be twenty to three because he liked the sound those words made on his lips, he finally slept, the almost empty bottle easing from his fingers until it half rested on the floor, the dying firelight dancing inside it as it rocked to and fro with the rhythm of his breathing, which was neither hopeful nor sad, but simply living.

At about four a small fall of soot smothered the flames, but the fire continued to smoulder, the gritty smoke rising from it, failing quite to reach to the high ceiling, and covering Smith, the armchair and the bottle in a fine veil of dark.

It was Jude he dreamed of, of the two of them in

another time. They were standing together under a spreading tree. He was pointing something out to her, and she was bending forward slightly so that her haunches sang for him.

She was wearing a dress the colour of old innocence, and her eyes were grey.

There was summer in the grass, and the ancient throb of bees in the deep wood.

She turned away from him, and laughed at something he had said, and forgotten.

Beside them, the lake had no colour, only the colours of all that surrounded it.

Smith was awakened by the bottle finally slipping from his fingers and clattering on the floor.

He opened his eyes like a man who has fallen asleep in one place and awakened somewhere else. Then he picked up the bottle, drank down the last of it, blew into it, and held his palm over the top, his eyes closed and his fingers supporting his chin.

He rose stiffly, leaving his outline behind in the soot-covered chair, and walked through the kitchen to the back door, which lay open to the dawn. It was not quite warm and not quite freezing, and all the snow had gone.

It is Christmas Day, he thought, and I am left with an empty bottle and an empty bed.

His face and his clothes had taken on the colour and sheen of graphite, and from the unswept garden a small paper bag came clambering up on the damp wind, leaving a tear in the perfection

of his left cheek on its way to the throbbing
gunmetal sky.

What was in Jude's mind, he thought, as she
stood here and tied a rope around the neck I kissed
so many useless times? What were her thoughts,
as she looked up at this sky?

What terrors passed through your mind, Jude, as
you walked down this path, that you could not
open this door and stand here for me, alive?

What a hum of resonance you would have given
to all the dead and silent objects which clutter up
this morgue of a house; the books and vases and
aching prints.

Even my stove has died. Its knobs sit there
accusing me, like the eyes of an old stuffed dog,
covered in dust.

There is dust on everything. I am sorry for that,
but what is the point in cleaning anything? I will be
as gone as you are before sooner becomes later,
and let all the dust gather on our eyelids then, let
it gather as it will.

Gone, gone, Jude. I wish with all my empty
heart, as I wished on the champagne bottle not half
an hour ago, that there was some miracle way of
unruining the way life turns out, of untying the
twisted certainty of it.

But there is too much dust in this room, in that

room. There is dust on my collection of Biggles books, which I once dusted every other day.

Things were always so easy for Biggles. There was nothing so irrevocable that it could not be undone with a quicksilver mind, the simple courage of the lion and the best of British luck.

But we are not allowed the obvious any more. Those of us who are left. We are not allowed the obvious, no matter how beautiful it is. It has been replaced by wit and cleverness, and all those useless things.

And Biggles is not here. I wish he was, so that I could tell him all this, and ask him what to do to bring you back. And then we could all go for a square meal at the Royal Aero Club, the three of us, and a well-earned spot of blanket drill.

But he is not, and you are not. There are only the rest of us, who cannot fly, and cannot fall.

I read last year of a woman who was making her first parachute jump. Her parachute opened, but she drifted into the blades of a helicopter. I wondered then what her thoughts were, when she knew she was going to die.

We are all sure of that, but not with the certainty of watching your feet drop into scything blades or feeling the noose tighten on your neck as the sky closes.

Perhaps there was no sky for you, Jude. Just this door into darkness, and me beyond it.

My sweet dead angel. How bloodless you were when I lifted you down. You hadn't been looking after yourself, at all.

And then the funeral. I wish your family had let me cremate you. There is more glory in flames and an ancient sojourn with the clouds than turning into sewage in a box.

You would have looked good at your funeral, Jude, with your black calf-length skirt clinging to your buttocks, your nipples thumbing through a rusty charcoal pullover.

And yet we were miserable and mad, that last year when we seemed to draw the insanity out of each other like leeches clinging face to face. How have I forgotten all that? How have I forgotten everything except how much it matters now that I will never see your face looking up at me, my love and anger and bitterness and madness all reflected candles guttering in your eyes? Jude?

Nothing. No Jude.

Just the caverns into which I plunged, plugged with cold wax and lukewarm maggots, like ears deaf to my cry for your return.

Damn you, Jude, for not listening to that cry, for leaving me alone when you were the only person who could have helped me through your death, for making me want you and then denying me that want with your final revenge, turning the body on which I weaned obsession into a foyer for the pettiest of carrion passing through. Worms in your eyes, and grubs inside you, where I once suckled divinity. Damn you, Jude, for that final, unbending, irretrievable revenge.

I am in that dark doorway, now, between two rooms. From one there comes the jive and chatter of popular music on someone else's radio, and from the other there comes the sound of nothing. The sound of a man waiting, waiting to play jazz saxophone in a cellar, and be an icon of beauty to women who are only passing through.

I am there now, Jude, and I have searched in many boxes in our attic, and now I hold what I am looking for, in my cold hand.

I have heard it said, somewhere or other, that no matter how long you hold a gun, it will never warm to the touch.

Smith sat in the cold armchair, the revolver in his lap and five bullets in the chamber. He had not found the sixth.

In his last dream, he and Jude were walking at first on wide, rolling slopes of green, and then in a forest.

And then, as they came into a clearing with a lake, hailstones came out of the blue sky, so that within a minute everything was white — the still surface of the lake, the grass at their feet, the diadems in her hair.

As he watched, the gems in her hair became water again, and she was human.

They lay down and slept close by, their toes touching like the blind love offerings of twins in the womb.

Smith woke then, and imagined for a while that he could still hear the breathing of Jude beside him.

When he was sure that he could not, he lifted the

revolver and placed it to the side of his brow.

There was nothing, in all the world. No sound, no word. There was only the letter o, which the barrel made on the hard flat flesh in which a tiny vein was beating, silent.

A small, empty sound, the o, waiting to be filled.

He pulled the trigger, a quarter of a second before the doorbell rang.

Smith is dead, thought the lawyer's wife. And I was not there to say anything or to hold him, so that he did not think I had deserted him when he needed someone so badly.

I am sorry, Smith, for all the times I brought you my trouble instead of my love.

Sorry that we made love so indifferently, the last time I saw you.

Were you asking for help, Smith, then, when you laid your head, still and silent, in the hollow of my arm?

But I held your head, and you did not answer, you did not move. Oh Smith, what more did you want, what more could I do?

The lawyer reached across the bed and took her hand.

'Poor Smith,' he said.

'Yes, poor Smith.'

'He didn't seem to have a great life.'

'Och, he had some good times,' she said, not

caring what her husband thought or felt.

They were silent for a time.

'We'll have a son, soon,' said the lawyer, chartless in uncertain waters, sending out distress flares into the fearful dark.

'Yes,' said the lawyer's wife. A little boy who we have already decided to call Solomon, who will come home from school every day with an expression that will make me want to say 'Had a hard day at the classroom, dear?' An expression of wisdom and suffering, of the burden of his name, as if life was something to be borne.

Like all men. Except Smith, who does not have to bear that burden any more.

Godspeed, Smith, she thought, and then the tears finally came.

'I want you to do something for me, Wolf,' Smith said afterwards. She lay naked beside him, her body like granite and flesh from his dust, so that together they looked like an undiscovered Rodin.

'A telephone call. Now that I am dead, we have to tell someone.'

She looked at him, but did not answer, then took the piece of paper from his hand and walked out of the room.

When she came back, seed pearls of sweat shone through the grey of her shoulder.

'Did she believe you?'

'It was the lawyer,' she said, lying beside him.

He kissed her shoulder, tonguing it until the flesh returned, then noticed the envelope in her hand.

'I found it,' she said, 'under the mat by the door.'

Smith shook the dust off it and tore it open. Inside was a slip confirming the lodgement in his bank from the lawyer, for the work.

'How thin you have become,' said Wolf, touching his belly with her fingernails until he thought she would draw blood.

Smith lay there, trying to remember whether it was the click of the empty chamber or the doorbell that had made him jump.

His body was on fire, and in his mind the past boiled in mist. He turned in the bed, twisting away from her.

'Smith,' said Wolf, 'we have all the time.'

He turned again, holding her near, his thigh between hers and their lips breathing close, so that his words did not reach her ears, but went in through her mouth, to her heart, there.

'Touch me,' he said. 'Touch me. We are going away, Wolf, and everything will be different.'

His voice was deeper than it had ever been, as sad and seductive as saxophone music in a church.

What he was saying became indistinguishable from the way he was saying it.

Touch me, said the humming in the air, the low resonance from the roof above their heads, even the light on the bed.

Wolf touched him, inside, in many colours, of a dark and bitter red, of blood and earth and liquid fire. All the colours he would ever need, from her.

'It is snowing outside, in the forest,' he said. 'There is no life in the forest, no colour, except the green almonds that open and close, which are the eyes of wolves, waiting, patient, hooded and bright.

'They are calling to each other, calling and calling as they hunt for their souls, calling for ever that their souls would come back to them.'

He looked down at Wolf, but she was asleep.

He leaned across and placed his hand on her rising and falling breast.

Outside, the echoes of the forest touched the window as gently as the love that keeps itself for corpses, then crept away again.

On St Stephen's Day they went out walking, nervous and reborn. The sky was nervous, too, blue cotton sheets torn to shreds and patched with clouds, threaded through with jet-trail silk.

He wanted Wolf walking beside him, a simple song in the rhythm of her feet.

They went for a drink, but he did not like it there. He was sure that someone would see him, and destroy his life now that it was over.

There were two other couples there, in the bar of the hotel they went to. There was a woman who wanted to go to bed with a man. She was trying with her animation to disguise the fact that she was not pretty, and had three fawn hairs growing out of her chin. He held a paperback book in his left hand and drank red wine with the other, gazing around indolently.

But he was not quite sure he was handsome. Occasionally, he was forced to look at her, sipping praise from her eyes as she tried harder and harder to seduce him.

There was also a cautious man in a beautiful black suit. He was with a woman who smoked cigarettes and looked around a lot, but he was in another world, beyond all those old feelings that people play with.

Smith took the lawyer's lodgement slip out of his pocket and made a note on it, then suggested to Wolf that they go.

That morning he had asked her what she had told her husband.

'That I was leaving him,' she had said, surprised at the question.

Now, as they left their drinks and walked away, she asked him what he had been writing on.

'Paper,' he said, and she laughed.

It was only when they were almost home that he realised the man in the black suit and the woman with him were the couple he had seen at the bus stop outside the café on the afternoon he had first met the lawyer's wife.

Everywhere the world wrestles with its shadow, he thought. Where had he read that?

had lit the fire in the old bedroom, Jude, and aired the white duvet cover, and our pillowcases like the egos of peacocks.

I could not even remember, as I tossed the white cotton high and let it settle, whether that room was your idea or mine.

A room of complete simplicity, I had told you — or you had told me — the floor bleached and the walls the colour of old hessian.

The wooden bed we had made by the carpenter we met in the country that scattered August day. Our serendipity bed, in the Christlike woods of ash and oak.

Do you remember the day we had it finished, Jude? The whole room bleached and drained as if by two thousand years of sun and salt, so that the arrogance of those pillows would have made you weep, one way or the other.

But then, I do not believe in rooms any more.

Wolf did not say a word. She crept in, curled up

on the bed and slept for an hour or more, as if she had been born there.

As if, if I rolled her over in her sleep, I would find the blue-grey stains of neglected afterbirth.

I allowed Wolf into the room, Jude, because I fear sin but need salvation more.

I allowed Wolf into the room, Jude, because I know she and you would have got on well, circling each other with the wary certainty of consequential futures, then giggling and discussing trips to penny markets.

Perhaps I let her in because you left me alone, Jude, and it has never been our room since then.

Or perhaps I let her in because we are going away tomorrow, to the land where the mountains are only a day away.

When she woke, I opened the other bottle of champagne from Christmas Day, losing the cork somewhere in the higher shadows of the room, and we undressed each other in front of the fire, piece by piece, stopping every so often to touch glasses and fingertip the dapples on our skin.

She wore a black dress. Lace underthings. A pair of black shoes. I laughed, that anyone could go out for the evening wearing so little and be covered up so chaste.

I loved watching the shadows move on her face

when she sucked me there, holding back her hair to see the silent fury of her cheekbones.

The tiny curve of her belly. The way she came, with a little question mark of surprise.

'It is good to have a fire in this room,' I said, before she slept.

'Or three,' she said.

Oh Wolf, you are wiser than you look.

Jude would have loved you, and hated you, too.

And now she lies beside me, her tawny head on my shoulder and her breathing more real than daytime dreams.

How I love Wolf's breathing. It is a steady wind that keeps the fragile kite of my hopes aloft.

Outside, the rain attempts once more to storm the windows, and fails.

There is just enough left in the bottle, Jude, for a wish for you. Just enough for a single drop to fall into the glass with a sound like a pebble falling on a stony plain, on the smallest star of a most distant galaxy.

A wish for you, Jude, that you are at peace at last, wherever you are, my oldest love.

I blow out the bedside candle, after a final look at Wolf, and lie down to sleep.

In the cluttering fireside darkness, I hold my

images of you and Wolf up before me and try to join the edges where they are torn and burnt.

But the past and the present will not match any more, and for that, at least, I have reason to hope there will be a future.